A Tuesday
Like Today

Other works by Cecilia Urbina

Fiction

Las locuras breves (1986)
La ruta de los cometas (1991)
Firme compañera (1994)
La imaginación de Roger Donal (1998)
De noche llegan (1999)
Un martes como hoy (2004)

Criticism / Nonfiction

El macho y la mujer moderna, como Julia Beltrán (1997)
De escritos y escritores (2001)

A Tuesday Like Today

Cecilia Urbina

Translated from the Spanish by
Clare E. Sullivan

WingsPress
San Antonio, Texas
2008

A Tuesday Like Today

Originally published as *Un martes como hoy*
by Fondo de Cultura Económica (© 2004)
Carretera Picacho-Ajusco 227, CP 14200, Mexico, D.F.

Cover print, "Night & Day" © 1997 by Arleen Polite

First Wings Press Edition

ISBN-10: 0-916727-47-5
ISBN-13: 978-0-916727-47-5
paperback original

Wings Press
627 E. Guenther
San Antonio, Texas 78210
Phone/fax: (210) 271-7805

On-line catalogue and ordering: www.wingspress.com
All Wings Press titles are distributed to the trade by
Independent Publishers Group
www.ipgbook.com

This publication was made possible in part
by a generous grant from the City of San Antonio,
Office of Cultural Affairs.

Library of Congress Cataloging-in-Publication Data

Urbina, Cecilia.
[Martes como hoy. English]
A Tuesday like today / Cecilia Urbina ; translated from the Spanish by Clare Sullivan.
p. cm.
ISBN 978-0-916727-47-5 (alk. paper)
I. Sullivan, Clare E., 1967- II. Title.
PQ7798.31.R35T8413 2008
863'.64--dc22
2008037643

Contents

To my three fellow travelers,
Jorge, Jorge Alberto and Cecilia,
witnesses to the birth of this novel
at the bar of the Grand Hotel in Angkor.

Translator's Preface

Translating *Un martes como hoy* afforded me a privilege not every translator enjoys, that of working in close partnership with an author. Cecilia Urbina was a "dream" collaborator for many reasons, her openness to questions, and particularly her excellent English. Cecilia's English is so perfect that at times I found myself wondering why she was even bothering to engage a translator! Being such a meticulous student of language, she frequently anticipated my questions before I even asked them, aware as she was of Spanish constructions that had no obvious counterparts in English. Yet all my inquiries were welcomed, from the most nitpicky to the dare-I-say personal. Such an easy rapport made the translation process both an easier and more enjoyable exploration of the intricacies of her thought.

Un martes como hoy is a story that traverses many landscapes. The opening finds the main characters (three Mexican nationals) in the jungles of modern Cambodia, telling tales of travels to the American Old West. The range of scenery and subject matter kept me on my toes to say the least. Over the year it took me to translate *Un martes como hoy,* I researched subjects as diverse as the Vietnam War, the ruins of Angkor and Spaghetti Westerns. At times I felt as ignorant as Camila and her husband Bobby when Márgara sets out to make their travel plans:

> "Now it's my turn to choose," spat Márgara. "We're going to Cambodia."
>
> "Africa is too far," said Bobby.

"And there's a war there," said Camila.
"It's not Africa and there's no war," she said and she disappeared in search of a guidebook.

Oh, right. I knew that.

Having had to traverse such varied terrain, I can offer advance warning to you the reader: that Cecilia plans to put you through your paces as well. For while this book entertains and engages, it also demands. Specifically, that one open one's eyes to the wide world, with all its disparate peoples, traditions, religious notions and politics. She won't be content for you to walk away merely amused.

One of the many reasons I'm so pleased to be able to translate this novel into English is because its history lessons are relevant to English-speaking audiences. Among them the human consequences of war, especially the Vietnam War and the bombing of Cambodia, made concrete and personal in the maimed bodies of the beggars the three main characters meet in the causeway of the temples of Angkor. But of course not all of Cecilia's history has such a pointed political statement to make. Indeed the tale our characters tell by night is a pop Western, filled with characters and dialogue that will no doubt be more familiar to English speaking audiences than readers of the original Spanish. "[W]hat you're getting is a rehash of all the cowboy movies I've ever seen in my life." (114), the character David says in the final pages of the book. And indeed, when it comes to scenes of cowboys riding off into the hackneyed sunsets, most of us are experts.

Is Urbina poking fun at us all in these pages? It's possible, since as well as being incisive and witty, I also know her to be a woman of great and generous humor. However it's my belief that ultimately she very much relies on the broad education of her readers, as her countless references, from Chaucer to Marguerite Duras to Millais and Rossetti, attest.

All of which is not to say that all there is to *Un martes como hoy* is subtext. For indeed it is Urbina's imagery that truly makes this novel come to life. As a lover and frequent translator of poetry, I was delighted to be presented with the challenge of translating her pictures into English. Interestingly, many of Urbina's images are literal snapshots: the glimpses of our three tourists' cameras as they travel from one locale to another. All are exquisite, more like paintings than photographs. The majesty of the temple at Ta Prohm, for example, its ruins intertwined with the roots of ancient banyan trees to such an extent that nature and architecture are indistinguishable. This theme, of the connection between nature and humanity is reiterated in her portrayal of the community of Siem Reap, a watery village that coexists with the Tonle Sap River and the lake of the same name, their houses built on pontoons. Ever since my initial reading in Spanish, her image of lake meeting sky with small boats of humans somewhere in between has stayed with me (I only hope I've managed to do it justice).

Urbina is likewise an artful manipulator of story, especially tension (as when a former Khmer Rouge hides menacing among the ruins with a rifle) as well as pain and pathos (in her depiction of an armless girl with a begging bowl clutched between her feet). In all instances, my challenge was to take it all in and render it with the faithfulness of a copy machine, doing everything I could to not mar the originals. I sought to capture emotion, yet not to add any of my own interpretations in the process.

A particular challenge at the very center of the book was to capture the three principal characters in English. They are all, to one extent or another, world travelers, and presumably spoke English reasonably well (this is revealed when they first met in a hotel bar and exchanged greetings without realizing that they are all Mexican). However they are also three distinct characters, each formed by their unique histories, culture and idiosyncrasies. In each instance I sought to listen closely to their voices, and choose diction and expressions that would set them apart from one another, particularly the two sisters who, though they were raised in the same household, have completely different personalities, views of themselves as social beings, and relationships to the third member of the love triangle, David. Speaking of whom, it is in fact David's personal quest that forms the heart of the plot. He himself can frequently sound preachy and pedantic when he lectures the sisters about politics or life. How to bring these personalities to life in English for my readers?

In this quest, my husband Jim was indispensable. A tireless editor, he reminded me again and again that, "No one would say that in English!" And I needed that reminding, since over the course of reading and re-reading these pages of words aloud, I frequently got too close to the literal meanings of the original text. Given that, I hope and trust I have done justice to this story and its characters for you, the reader in English. If I have, I must also thank my editor Bryce Milligan for his support of the project and his understanding during the process and my colleagues Mary Makris, Rhonda Buchanan, and David Anderson for taking an interest in my work.

– Clare E. Sullivan
University of Louisville
Louisville, Kentucky

Angkor

T**he temples of Angkor** have been fixed in my imagination ever since I can remember, obsessing me with their mysterious smiles. The Khmer smile. When I first saw them in the pages of books, floating on the faces of the statues in the Guimet Museum in Paris, I told myself I would go to Angkor if it were the last thing I ever did. But then wars closed Cambodia off to me. Angkor became a chimera.

Until now.

Just a few years ago, visiting the temples of Angkor was an adventure. Armed deserters roamed the ruins. Signs warned travelers about buried mines. Siem Reap was a ghost town, and finding anything to drink was a near impossibility. Now I see tourists—however few—taking over the colonial splendor of the Grand Hotel, driving around in climate-controlled SUVs, and I feel like a foreigner. A foreigner in the Cambodia that I know so well. Or maybe 'stranger' is a better word. I know things visitors couldn't possibly learn, except maybe by reading newspapers, which they only do from a great distance, with their characteristic air of civilized disbelief. I am here, among them, an unwanted witness. But I go back, again and again, because I can't stay away.

Angkor Thom

They met him in the bar of the Grand Hotel: one of those people you only glimpse for a moment, whose image leaves no trace, but who reappears later like a ghost in some photograph. He sat down at the piano, taking the place of a French woman whose songs filled the place with nostalgia. The Grand Hotel seemed to have missed decades of history. It ignored the massacres, the exodus and the hate, and stayed behind in a colonial daze, in a time when the tributaries of the Mekong flowed uninterrupted from the ocean down to the rice fields. Márgara longed for a chiffon dress, a hat with flowers, and a Chinese lover from Cholen. The pianist's voice took her to another time. Such is the evocative power of music when the allusions are familiar.

"Play it again, Sam," someone said from a nearby table. And he did, just like he always did when a request came his way. At least until the hotel's strict dinner hour prevailed and the guests marched off to the dining room. He played a few more bars:

"Thank you for your indulgence—and for allowing me to trespass on this piano bench."

Camila, who'd been half-listening, reacted. Her glance shot to the piano like an arrow and hit the poor fellow right between the eyes. Camila's look never fails. In no time his voice was silenced and he appeared at our table.

"David Masters-Iturbe," he said.

"Are you a professional singer?" Camila asked in English.

"Oh no, very much an amateur," he responded, also in perfect English.

He gestured for permission to join them, then asked if they were tired from their trip, from which they deduced he'd been living at the hotel long enough to be able to pick out new guests. He paused a long while, waiting for one of them to continue the conversation, which Camila did, initiating a defense of his "amateur" musical abilities.

"We'll be late for dinner," Márgara interrupted in Spanish. David Masters-Iturbe looked up with a start.

"Where are you from?" he asked in Spanish.

"Mexico."

"Frankfurt."

"We flew in from Frankfurt, but we're from Mexico," Márgara explained.

"What a coincidence! I'm Mexican too. And all this time we've been talking English."

"In a place like this . . ."

"I thought you were British. Or American. You sing like a New Yorker."

"I lived in New York for years. But don't let me keep you. As you said, you're going to be late for dinner."

You never get a traveler's identity quite right. Being in a foreign land dissolves boundaries and lumps individuals together under a generic, tourist label that has a way of suppressing individual personalities. Afterwards I asked Camila where she had thought David was from: American, she said, because of the songs. Australian, I said. Why Australian? Because he has the look of someone who spends a lot of time outside, brown hair burnished by the sun . . . or, because I don't know many Australians.

We all went on to the dining room, since for David Masters-Iturbe it didn't seem necessary to ask permission. He sat down at our table with a natural ease. For two hours

I watched a mutual seduction play itself out. Despite his unfortunate name, he had what it took to wage a proper campaign. His smile caught my attention, a little to one side, as if he did it with only one part of himself, and the rest took a while to catch on. His gaze darted back and forth, hypnotized by Camila. It leapt occasionally back to me, in a vain attempt to be fair. In hindsight what I remember from that night is his smile, which remained in the air like the Cheshire cat's after I got tired and went to bed. Camila came in quite a bit later. When she did I caught a threatening *see you tomorrow*.

"Camila, you're crazy. Are we going to drag that guy around with us all day?" I protested as soon as she closed the door.

"Don't be that way. He's interesting."

"He may or may not be as interesting as you think, but I don't like the idea of visiting temples with a stranger."

"You're so selfish. You know how many times David has been to Cambodia? Thousands. He knows more about this country than anyone."

"*No one* has been to this country thousands of times, not in the last few years anyway."

"Well he has."

"So what is he then, an archeologist, a reporter, a doctor without borders, a mercenary?

"No nothing like that. He's got a paper-making business."

"Makes sense, I suppose. Wars in Cambodia are fought with paper airplanes."

"You're so sarcastic. You're going to love him. Anyway, you're the one who likes Angkor so much."

That night I almost couldn't sleep. The anticipation of something I'd waited so long to see made me toss and turn in my bed in the kind of fog that makes things seem bigger than they are. Ten minutes before landing in Siem Reap, Camila had asked me:

"Are you sure there isn't a war?"

"These days you can't ever be sure. But don't worry, nothing happens to tourists."

"That's not true, Márgara. I read that in Egypt a bunch of people died."

I didn't want to comment on what happens to tourists in cases like that. Travelers have a tendency to think of themselves as invulnerable, as though they occupy an alternative space where local events don't affect them. That's always been my impression, and I wished that it were true, especially since I was feeling responsible for having brought Camila to a country with a precarious political situation. I dreamt a mish-mash of warriors and temples in a jungle that had been invisible until now. And David Masters-Iturbe's smile.

He busies himself with coffee while he waits for them to come down to breakfast. Earlier he'd cancelled the SUV that would have picked them up at the hotel and taken them to the temples, and instead has his jeep ready at the entrance. At the time it didn't seem like such a presumptuous thing to do; at least from what Márgara had said they didn't want a guide, though he was prepared to fill the role just in case. He was seduced by the idea of seeing through their eyes what he already knew so well. They arrived wearing khaki shorts, sunglasses, and thick-soled shoes. Travelers ready for an adventure. They could be twins, Márgara a dark-haired contrast; seeming older, even though she's the single one . . . older and more thoughtful. Her sister with a power of seduction that could be either cynical or innocent, he still couldn't decide. But it had been a while since he'd felt such an immediate attraction to a stranger . . . or that a stranger had seduced him so deliberately. Her look was an unmistakable invitation that he answered, only to find himself presented with two very different possibilities . . . new elements in the complex equation that was his return trip.

Each time Camila sets out to make a man fall in love with her she does it, though her ability has always outstripped her judgment. All through high school, college and the years after, while her friends got married Camila kept on collecting predictable failures.

"I just met the most wonderful man," she announced to her sister one night. "His name is Bobby, he came right up to me at the party and told me: I saw you from a distance and decided that you're the woman I'm going to marry."

"You mean you just met an imbecile," Márgara answered and went back to sleep.

The man was prescient though: he did marry her and in the bargain proved he was no imbecile. In any case, he was a person of means—as ample as they were inexplicable—generous to his wife and, by extension, her family. Because of him, they were both in Angkor. When his ill-defined business called him to Frankfurt in the middle of winter, he decided to bring Camila along and to invite Márgara, who was recovering from the failure of a magazine that she'd launched with such high hopes. Her magazine as well as her partner (likewise a vessel of her expectations) had failed to live up to their promise. Come with us, Bobby proposed; spend a little time with Camila while I work and you'll perk back up.

"Frankfurt in January. Thanks, but I think I'd rather be depressed in a different climate."

"Come on, Márgara, that way I won't have to be alone while Bobby works, and then we can go to Paris."

The word Paris was key. And when Bobby works he literally disappears. He wasn't made for schedules; no nine to five, or ten. He makes his appointments at six in the morning or at one; he'll take the day off and move around at night like a vampire. His time is suspended in a space unknown to mortals. The whole family—with more or less discretion—has pointed it out to Camila, but she's impervious to doubt; businessmen don't have a schedule, she'd say, but decline to elaborate on what kind of business it is that requires its executives to be in attendance at dawn.

Their week in Frankfurt stretched to three and threatened to get longer, while Camila and Márgara ran out of indoor activities and shivered in the dark at three in the afternoon, contemplating foggy streets and the frozen breath of pedestrians.

"It's no use waiting for me," Bobby finally declared in the face of their dissatisfaction. "I have no idea how much longer I have to stay. You might as well go somewhere else for a while."

"Now it's my turn to choose," spat Márgara. "We're going to Cambodia."

"Africa is too far," said Bobby.

"And there's a war there," said Camila.

"It's not Africa and there's no war," she said and she disappeared in search of a guidebook. Once the precise location of Cambodia had been established, Bobby had no more objections (his personal aversion to Africa is something we'll have to talk about another time) and Camila let herself be seduced by the brochures of Angkor's Grand Hotel and the need to acquire proper attire, not an easy task in the middle of a European winter. "Why don't we shop in Bangkok?" she offered with enthusiasm.

The road to Cambodia was paved with a large quantity of shops and acquisitions, some of an exotic nature (among them a gigantic ancient Buddha) impossible to take along, which were consigned, properly packaged, to Frankfurt and Bobby's care.

It's said that from infancy we define ourselves as either auditory or visual beings. There are those who prefer to have the things they see explained to them; others prefer to read about them. So perhaps in this sense reading is equivalent to seeking. When someone tries to explain what I'm seeing to me, it's like listening to an analysis of a symphony while it is being performed. The ruins have their own tonality which requires silence to be transmited. And then there's the delicious option of losing yourself, of having to find your own way and thereby make your own discoveries.

I didn't get lost in Angkor Thom, at least not physically. Visitors were scarce; our hotel companions, mostly Europeans, neatly and promptly concluded their visits and disappeared immediately, probably in pursuit of the next item on the program. In silence I wandered the place, ignorant of the passage of time despite the height of the sun and the quietude.

They were there, their gaze lost over the horizon, looking out toward the four cardinal directions. Time is smoothing their features, imbuing their Khmer smile with increasing mystery. Their faces are becoming confused with the stone, from which they appeared to meditate with a certain irony on their former owners' destiny. For me, so obsessed with investigating the past, with anchoring what I see with dates and facts, consulting the guidebook held no interest. There'll be time for that later, when the figures start to lose their certainty and I need to recapture them in images or words. Was it a Bodhisattva or King Jayavarman VII who sought to immortalize himself in stone? I preferred to take them in without trying to decipher the message they've kept secret for centuries. Photographs, taken from every distance and angle, were what I needed to congeal the present.

I found them on the Elephant Terrace, sitting on the floor, enjoying a smoke and contemplating some vestige of an imperial hunt in the territory's shadowy jungles.

"It's about time you showed up," Camila said. "We thought you'd been carried away by the ghost of some Khmer."

"Almost. This place doesn't need ghosts to carry me away . . . even the ones you feel floating around in here."

David looked at me.

"I guess the magic's had its effect. And there's so much left. . . . Want to continue the journey this afternoon?"

"I'd rather go tomorrow. I need some time. . . ."

"Time to let yourself feel it. I know what you mean."

We went back to a swimming pool the size of a reservoir to relax in the cool waters after the heat of the day. So much leaping in time, from the twelfth century to the 1920s (since that's about where I'd place this hotel) or anywhere but now, in 1999, leaves us in no time at all. Here there's nothing to remind me of an airplane, a telephone, the Frankfurt cold or my apartment in Mexico. And then there's this character we've just acquired, this David Masters-Iturbe, who's made our trip for two into a threesome. He belongs in a movie, some solitary nomad on an Asian trail.

"You're such a jerk, Márgara. Going off on your own and not listening to David's stories."

"I don't know, I think she's got the right idea," he said. "Maybe there's a better time for stories."

It bothered me that he'd assumed a job he hadn't been given, stealing our time and organizing it like a teacher with his pupils. I saw no way of saying it without offending him; but then the worst thing that could happen is that the original duo just swaps elements. And that didn't seem so terrible, honestly. Some experiences are more fulfilling when you're alone.

Later, on the veranda, brandy in hand, the clear night reflected in the pool, David's words don't seem so ominous. He has a beautiful voice—she'd already noticed it while he was at the piano—and a certain storyteller's charm. He picks up the guidebook they brought and leafs through it, pausing at the maps and photographs.

"You picked a good edition. This woman has written quite a few books on the art and culture of Southeast Asia. She knows more than any tour guide."

"I don't like traveling with a guide."

"Yeah I noticed. But it's the sad state of modern tourism. The only way to get to know a country, or a city, or a ruin, is to wander alone, or in good company: someone who's got similar interests or who at the very least can leave you to explore on your own."

"As long as you don't mention the word tourist . . . that word makes me think of some docile flock that won't call a building a cathedral until someone tells them to."

"You should trust your own spontaneous impressions. You'll give me yours I'm sure . . . and your sister will too. It's a land filled with mystery . . . You'll see quite a few images of Buddha, the entire Hindu epic carved on the temple wall, but don't be fooled. Originally the people of this country were animist and magical. They still have cults to the local spirits, the inhabitants of the rivers, the trees, the mountains, the stones. Those phantoms Márgara mentioned, the ones floating among the ruins, who knows? They might be the spirits of the rock, trapped by the sculptors, prisoners of the bas-reliefs. You can almost see the *asparas* sometimes, the celestial nymphs, dancing. . . . Legend has it that the Khmers were the descendants of Kamu, the mythical ancestor of Preh Thong, who abandoned India and set sail for Cambodia. One night he met a beautiful *nagini* at the seashore, fell instantly in love and married her. The girl's father was the king of the *nagas*—serpent-gods who live in the underworld, or beneath the sea, who control rain and prosperity. You can see them along all the avenues that lead to temples, standing there like protective guardians. Seeing how happy his daughter was, the king drank up all the water that was covering the land, built a capital and gave the country, which he called Kambuja, to the newlyweds."

"Serpent-gods instead of sirens . . ."

"But enough about history. Tell me about yourselves."

"I'm afraid we'll seem rather boring compared to those legends."

"Let's start with your names. I've never met another Márgara."

"Do our names seem that unusual to you?"

"A person gets a name for a reason, because of their parents, their grandparents, maybe someone's secret love . . . there's always a story behind it."

"Camila was our great-grandma's name and that really is a story. There's a long series of Camilas in our family. They may skip a generation or two, but eventually they always come back. Most of them don't have stories attached to them, at least as far as I know, but great-grandma is something of a household myth. Her notoriety came from her husband Francisco, the kind of fellow who would stand out in any ancestral cabinet of curiosities. Our grandmother always insisted that Camila—that one there, that you are looking at—looked like great-grandma. No one took her seriously until she dug out a photograph and showed it to us: green eyes (the photograph is black and white, but you can tell they're light-colored), that nose, her thick lips, the kind that probably weren't in fashion back then, are quite similar. That was back when my sister wore her hair extremely long and we teased her by calling her Rapunzel. Fortunately everyone in our family (even grandmother) is rather sensible, so reincarnation never occurred to any of them, though they say that Camila has more in common with her than the color of her eyes or the shape of her nose."

"What for instance?"

"My grandmother made it all up! Márgara just likes telling everyone that," Camila jumped in. "But then, that's not her name. It's Margarita, but I'm sure you've noticed how stubborn she is. Being the oldest I remember how angry she used to get when people called her that. 'Treating me like a baby,' she used to say. Everyone told her Margarita isn't a baby name, that it's the name of a flower, but she bugged my mother so much that one day she finally said, 'Okay, you can be Márgara.' Now the only place you can find the name Margarita is in her passport, if at all."

"A rose by any other name . . ."

"Yours isn't so common either, Mr. Masters-Iturbe. . . . With a hyphen, I suppose?"

"Yes. I have my grandfather to thank for it. He was British and thought that adding his wife's last name would help his children feel at home in their new country."

He found the fraternal squabbles amusing. Is that what you call it when you're talking about women? He had no idea what to think of all the competitive baggage they carried. An heir to who-knows-what virtues from a great-grandma and a little girl who refused to be infantilized by a name. . . . This forced waiting, at times so frustrating, can have its rewards. . . .

"How long do you plan to stay in Siem Reap?"

Márgara glanced at her sister inquiringly.

"Camila? What do you think?"

"I don't know. It all depends on my husband. Or on us, if he spends too long in Frankfurt. What do you think?"

"I'd like to stay here as long as we can, live it all a little. I've dreamt of this place for so long. I don't want it to be like a movie that goes by too fast . . ."

"If you want to stay a few days, you ought to know there's no nightlife. The hotel, the bar, the pool . . . do you play cards?"

"Not really, we talk about the game while we play and drive all the serious players nuts. You?" asked Camila.

"I was a 'serious' player, as you say, for a time. Maybe that's why I don't like the game anymore."

"If it's late night fun we want, we can get Márgara to tell us stories," Camila says. "You can't imagine how she used to entertain us as girls, our whole circle of friends."

"An excellent idea," says David. "What kind of stories? Horror, romance?"

"Oh, nothing like that. All I did was repeat my grandmother's tales, all of which are quite preposterous. But they've become a kind of family mythology. Camila knows them as well as I do," added Márgara.

"Well, let's get to know your grandmother then. What do you say?"

"I agree, provided it's a fair exchange. We'll all have to tell stories. You know a lot about this country, for example."

"I'll have to think about that. I'm sure something will come to me. What about you, Camila?"

"I'm not that creative, but I'm good at reading between the lines, figuring out the untold story. I know my grandmother too, like Márgara said."

"Well then. We'll have to secure some refreshments for the long night ahead."

"Like the characters on the road to Canterbury?" Márgara joked.

"Why not? We're in the same situation. We're all here, having met by chance on the road, in a place that's fascinating by day but too quiet by night. What better opportunity to use our imaginations? Call it a challenge: whoever comes up with the best story wins a champagne dinner on the last night. The others treat."

"Alright. Then I'm going to tell the story of a great-grandma, maybe ours, maybe someone else's, exactly the way it was told to me. Camila can either pick up where I leave off, or come up with something else. And you, you'll have to use your imagination.

"So. Once upon a time there was a grandmother . . . no, wait, that's not right. She'd have had no idea she was ever going to be a grandmother at that point. Let me start again, and I'll begin by saying that none of this has to be true. In the sole existing photograph of Camila Fuentes Ogarrio, she's playing with her half-braided hair, into which flowers and pearls are being woven, like a subject in a Pre-Raphaelite painting. My source (and by that I mean the person who told me this story) extols her legendary eyes, more yellow than green, and the love of her parents for their only daughter. He talks about how she met Francisco Videgaray, a very bad poet—as evidenced by his only surviving work, one more gallant than literary—but the possessor of a fiendishly seductive gaze.

Cousin Amelia was getting married. The wedding was the biggest thing to happen to Camila in all her fifteen years. Seamstresses whirled around her for weeks, adjusting her bodice, embroidering the ivory-colored chiffon that had caused her mother Belén such terrible grief. How could she wear a dress in that color? The bride and the bride alone is entitled to white, and no one has the right to upstage her. It was the first time Camila would attend an important event as an adult. A precarious adult, certainly, but that was back when women grew up fast and she wanted to look pretty. And though she didn't say it, even prettier than her cousin. Belén resorted to bribery: green brings out your eyes so nicely. A pale shade will also make the pearls stand out. For the same reason, both the pearls and the color of her dress were crucial to Camila. She had recently discovered a reproduction of *Ophelia*. It didn't matter to her that Ophelia was dead. The mysterious atmosphere of the painting had seduced her: flowers scattered about a floating body, and above all, a bodice embroidered with precious gems. That and only that was what she wanted to wear to her cousin's wedding. She wanted to be Ophelia . . . but alive. The photograph I was talking about bears witness to her triumph. In it she's wearing the ivory-colored dress with an embroidered bodice and flowers in her flowing hair.

"It all had the desired effect. She was prettier than Amelia. The stares of the young male guests confirmed this, though with the discretion that was proper to the age. Among the boys was Francisco Videgaray. He was utterly bored. My source doesn't actually make mention of him at this point in the tale, only his boredom. He wasn't very fond of those types of ceremonies. He was fond of very few things really, a peevish attitude that kept him on a tightrope as far as the family was concerned. He didn't yet deserve the term black sheep, but his hue was getting darker by the minute. His mother had brought him to the celebration, dragged him really, in hopes that contact with proper society would have a positive effect on him. And since Francisco was desperately in need of a few good marks in the family ledger, he let himself be led. He deposited his mother between two ancient aunts and fled to the garden to smoke. There he found Camila, hindered by an elaborate tangle of a thousand tiny pearls. Here my source is as forthright as he can be, given the strictures of his time. At no point does the term *coup de foudre* enter the story. Camila's mind was fixed on herself, on not tripping on her dress, which was longer than she was used to, on not wilting her flowers prior to her triumphant entry. Francisco watched the cigarette smoke fade away and didn't really think about anything. Doesn't the girl look darling, Belén said to herself, and with so many prospects! Camila's eyes ran up and down the dresses of the other guests (not one had a dress as beautiful as she) over to the matrons' jewels (but they would be unthinkable for an unwed young woman), the decorations in the room, the bride's smile, the groom's bearing (not tall enough), finally settling on the person of Francisco. The poor young fellow was standing in a corner, dispassionately regarding the guests as one might a flock of particularly uninteresting sheep.

"Camila's gaze caught his in the same way that my sister's caught yours. Remember though that our Camila, who is only the most recent in the line of Camilas, merely practices what others before her invented and perfected. Her great-grandma had to act on intuition, or possibly on an instinct she inherited from some other ancestor with the same abilities. The point is that Francisco might have done the same thing you did if it weren't for the fact that a nineteenth-century man was inhibited by other considerations. Thus he would have asked himself who could introduce him to that pretty girl with the golden eyes. He wasn't confident enough in any of the servants to ask for such a favor. His mother wasn't even an option. And so immediately, he would begin to weave a web destined to destroy him. He could send her a flower. What madness! The worst way to get noticed. Of course my source doesn't dare mention the concept of destiny. It was just one of those coincidences, so maddening to scientists, when two lines of inquiry converge at the same point and the same time. Francisco toyed with his image of himself as a poet, a daydream with little basis in reality, born from reading some book a friend with more poetic sensibilities had lent him. He did have a fine memory, but scant sense of literary etiquette, or aesthetics. Together, those traits impelled him to take up the wedding invitation his mother carried in her purse and write on the opposite side. . . ."

Then, barely containing their laughter, the two sisters recite in unison:

Your eyes peered from the shadows
Of the rushing of your hair
As in a shaded forest
One finds a clear pool there
I saw my heart reflected
In the gold hue of your eyes
So anxious then to hurl me
To the current of my sighs.

"Work in hand," continued Márgara "he crossed over to Camila and placed it beside her. In her surprise she started to say something, but he raised a finger to his lips, winked and withdrew. He watched her unfold the paper, read it several times, then cast her eyes about the room for him. This time she did not do it intuitively, but rather deliberately. Francisco was terrified. He had just committed every possible breech of etiquette: he had approached a proper young woman without having been introduced, written a love poem to a stranger at a family gathering, and worst of all, used words unfit for chaste and pristine ears. Of course he didn't consider the most serious of his crimes, the slaughter of a perfectly good poem by Rossetti. But Francisco wasn't burdened by superfluous feelings of remorse. What was causing his panic was that second glance: it showed she had accepted the poem's proposition and felt no shame. He didn't know what to do just then, but as it turned out, even if he'd wanted to do something, circumstances prevented it.

"Camila wasn't guilty of the shamelessness that so terrified Francisco (she just wasn't conscious of that gaze of hers), and the subsequent inquiries she made were completely innocent. It was one of her aunts who recognized the young fellow: Doña Edelmira Videgaray's son. 'I believe it's Francisco, the youngest of her boys.' When Camila looked around for him again he had disappeared. Still, she tucked the sheet of paper away and decided she had found the man of her dreams."

Márgara takes a long swig from her cocktail. The others watch, waiting for her to continue.

"And?" David asks.

"That's it for today. It's your turn. You've each got the same amount of time I took to tell your story."

"Hey that's not fair. You couldn't possibly have such a good memory, or an imagination like that. That poem you two recited together . . ."

"It's part memory and part creative whimsy. The two of us have heard the story so many times, and so many different ways. . . . At this point I don't know if what I'm saying is original or if I've been changing it as I go along. And I only know half of it."

"Well since we're stuck in the past, I think I'll tell the same story, only the way it was told to me," said Camila.

"That night, Camila, our supposed great-grandma, didn't go to the wedding by herself, like Márgara says. She went with her cousin Lucía who wasn't so flighty, probably because she was a little older. She wasn't wearing pearls, or flowers, or Ophelia's hairdo. When they came to get her and Lucia saw Camila she thought, I don't know who she's trying to be, but whoever it is it's worth the effort. She looks pretty. She probably also noticed the party dresses, the jewels, the gallant young men, the groom's bearing, and obviously the bored guy in the corner (they say Francisco was so good-looking that you couldn't help noticing him). My source doesn't say if she liked Francisco. Lucía was as tight-lipped as an oyster, so my source is probably a little less reliable. Her quiet ways made her a good observer of other people, none of that "looks could kill" stuff, just the good judgment to know when someone was interested in her, or in somebody else. She saw the looks (the ones that really could kill), and the poem exchange, the wink, and the fact that, having read the note, her cousin looked like she'd seen Don Juan in person. She (not the aunt) was the one who told Camila who the shy guy with the letter was, since she'd been to a lot of parties, and she'd met the Videgarays. Lucía had been to their hacienda quite a few times, and was a close friend of the older brother's girlfriend. She knew all about Francisco's highly questionable skills. She didn't say anything else because he'd disappeared after the whole poem episode—and why ruin it for the poor girl? Once she saw Camila sigh like some girl from a soap opera, fold the paper up twenty times and tuck it between her pearls, she decided not to say anything. But don't let that fool you. Her part in this story is a lot more important than you might think. But, if you don't mind, now I'm going to sleep."

"Wait, you can't. What about David?" Márgara protested.

"I already told you the story of the *nagas.* Besides, the truth is I'm scared. I don't think I can compete with you all. I shouldn't have been so bold."

"We have a deal, you. You've got no choice but to participate."

"Tomorrow then. Maybe I'll have a brilliant dream."

Preah Kan

Mornings in Angkor are bright and cool this time of year. I suggested they visit the smaller temples before going on to Angkor Wat. It's up to you, I said. It all depends on whether you want to come upon it slowly, and leave the surprise for the end, or see it right away and be dazzled. The first time I came here, it was years ago now, I was so afraid that something unexpected would happen and I'd be forced to leave, I took it in all at once, terrified I wouldn't get another chance. The next day, and over the course of many more, I looked at it again. I've come back here at the worst of times, when it was complete madness. Nowadays there are no more peaceful people than the small population that lives here, devoted to their daily tasks alongside their sleeping temples. Today there is no evidence of violence whatsoever on the little dirt roads, or in the wooded park in front of the hotel. Least of all in this one, preserved as it is as a vestige of times gone by.

Someone once said, I have seen more than I remember, but I remember more than I have seen. I don't want to remember Angkor as a series of isolated images, a puzzle that I can't put back together without photographs, which once I put in order and name, structure the experience in a way that your memory can't integrate. So you construct an imaginary journey in your mind, one you archive in an alternate reality from your day-to-day experiences. Yet if it so happens that experience and the photographic record correspond, then the humidity, smells and sounds merge with the images and envelop you. That's how I want to relive Angkor afterward—trapped on the pages of an album. So I vote for the long road. Let's start with the smaller temples, I say. We'll leave the big surprise for the end.

You can see Angkor Wat from the highway, a mirage reflected in a moat. It tests my resolve. But this country has more to offer than just one surprise. The main avenue into Preah Kan leads to the jungle, which hides the temple in a tangle of green.

"They say that Preah Kan was lost four hundred years ago," explains David, "and that a Cambodian king found the outer wall during an elephant hunt. But they say that about other temples too. The name means *sacred sword,* so maybe the jungle hid it away, in safe keeping for the descendents of the ancient kings. . . ."

The roots of centuries-old ceiba trees embrace the rocks, propping them up. Here I finally find the jungle, what I'd like to call *my* jungle, the one that's inhabited my dreams since I was a girl. Sea and jungle. Pirates and explorers. Livingstone searching for the source of the Nile. This Asian jungle is the myth that underlies all others. We are alone, immersed in four hundred invisible years. The king and his retinue of hunters have yet to arrive, though we can sense the light footsteps of the monks in the corridors, the smell of sacred incense. We arrive at *dharmasala,* which according to David was a refuge constructed for pilgrims. Would they be like Europeans? The ones on the road to Santiago? Or like the characters from the stories told by the bonfire on the way to Canterbury? Submissive pilgrims, their tired steps demanded of them by the gods. They traveled the docile prairies of England or the arid, Spanish paths. This would be a perilous way, where one was at the mercy of beasts, of a natural world capable of swallowing armies whole and leaving no trace. Are we the modern pilgrims?

I take a photo of Camila climbing the roots like a monkey.

David observes us through cigarette smoke with his eyes half closed. His pipe is for the evenings, from what I can tell. He returns to the jeep and brings back bottles of water and the oranges he carried off from the buffet this morning, improvising a picnic in the shade.

"I was thinking a moment ago about the pilgrims," Márgara says. "The ones who came to seek Buddha, enlightenment, I don't know . . . and I wonder just what it is we're looking for when we come here."

"Are we a modern version of the pilgrims, you mean?" David asks.

"Yes, exactly."

"I suppose so, in the sense that we're searching for something beyond the familiar. And not just to see it, but to live it. A little bit of the unknown."

"Something you couldn't find in a city like Hong Kong."

"A pilgrim can only search for the intangible."

"Like Angkor."

"Right, so let's call ourselves pilgrims of the past, of mystery."

"Did it ever occur to you two that we might just want to be somewhere else?" Camila's tone is impatient. "You start turning into a zombie when every day is the same. But being here we're different." We all fall silent. She notices the silence and gets up. "Well, enough of that. Where do we go now?"

They are in no hurry. The journey lacks structure or limits. While Bobby is freezing in the Nordic snows—

which he will probably continue to do, if his nightly calls are any indication—they can stay as long as they like. Camila would probably get impatient after a few days, maybe invent a trip to Bali or back to Bangkok. Fortunately David is here, and he acts like an anchor for her. His smile, his pipe and the trunk full of stories he tells at night are a passport to Angkor. Camila would see everything at once if she could, obsessively, only to end up worn out, ready for some other plane, some other country. It reminds Márgara of birthday parties when they were girls. Camila had to open all the presents, dress the doll, put the electric train tracks together, color in the coloring books. Say yes to all the boys. Maybe that's the tie that binds her to Bobby, the thing her family doesn't understand, his ability to put one surprise package after another in front of her, beginning with the first one: you are the woman I'm going to marry. What an irresistible proposition for an impatient imagination! Márgara observes her sister and her new friend. She wouldn't like to find herself trapped in the middle of a romance. She wouldn't pretend to be responsible for others, but she also doesn't want to have to tell her brother-in-law that his wife got lost in Cambodia. David distributes his attentions equally to both of them. That flirtation of the first night, when Camila's gaze drew him to her like a magnet, hasn't happened since. Márgara is aware of that power, so much so she'd even tried to practice it herself, first through her eyelashes, head bowed, raising her eyes slowly until they were fixed upon a man with such intensity that, for a second, he believed he just might be a genius. Yet her experiments invariably failed for one of two reasons: either she lost control and laughed at the key moment, just as the guinea pig was about to succumb, or, concentrating on a perfect performance, she failed to discern her target, discovering only later what an idiot he was. With age, she came to reject the use of those kinds of borrowed and potentially risky tactics, though deep down she suspected she'd wasted an invaluable resource.

They visit what might be called an ancient spa, a place devoted to beauty and luxury. "Oh, to have lived at such a time, a woman in an age that idolized women," David says, quoting an unknown source. "The men and their armies were drawn to the temples of Shiva the Powerful, but the princesses came to the temple of Neak Pean to make their offerings of wrought gold and perfume."

Do they really—or did they—idolize their women? Ancient inscriptions traced lineage and property matrilineally, and speak of women with political and economic power during the Angkor period. Are they mere tales or truths? It's possible that we no longer know how to idolize women. Perhaps we only idolize those things we've never had contact with. Perhaps we only fall in love with the unknown, with what we can't understand.

Leaving, we run into a group of Italians with their Cambodian guide. He's wearing a bright checkered bandana, the kind all the vendors try to sell you at the entrances to the monuments. They pick up on our interest and gather round: *one dollar, one dollar.* Everything costs the same: the bandanas, the carved figurines, the cans of Coke. It's a one-dollar economy, probably due to the difficulty of changing the local currency. Before long the bandanas are two for one. We have no idea how far the price might drop in accordance with the law of supply and demand. But at that particular moment supply and demand align and we buy one of every color: blue, green, red.

"Why red?" asks David.

"They're brighter, which must be why everyone seems to have one."

"Everyone like the Khmer Rouge, you mean? I don't care for the association." There's more seriousness in his tone than the topic seems to warrant.

From that moment on I can't help but notice the rectangle of lightweight cotton most of the inhabitants have around their necks. Almost everyone gets around by bicycle or moped, swerving gently this way and that to avoid pedestrians and automobiles as they putter about the city. Every time I see the red and white bandana I ask myself if it has any meaning. Could it be a former Khmer Rouge? Is it a matter of taste or ideology? The latter seems absurdly menacing to me. I don't want to ask David and alter the mood, the weary happiness we feel.

But that night Camila asks him anyway: "Why do red bandanas bother you?"

"They bring up bad memories. It's the symbol of a bizarre revolution that tried to erase Cambodia, or Kampuchea as they call it now, from history. Or perhaps I should say erase its own history. That tried to empty the cities and return it to a pastoral existence. Bizarre notions, as I said. Not intrinsically perverse, except for the fact that millions died. But then I suppose statistics aren't all that reliable," he adds to soften the effect.

"But it's only a matter of fashion now, isn't it? They come in so many different colors."

"Oh certainly, nowadays there may be no real reason for choosing red over blue or green. It just brings up bad memories, like I said. . . ."

"Personal ones?"

"Not exactly. Those of friends, who lived those terrible times. I come back to see the things that survived the war. The ruins and the people."

"Do you have a lot of friends here?"

"Some in Phnom Pen. Journalists and diplomats who

came back after the war. But that is not the Cambodia you came here to see."

"Do you plan to stay a long time?"

"I don't know. I can't go home now."

We can tell he'd rather not continue the conversation, so we go off to get ready for dinner.

"Did David tell you what he does for a living?" I ask back in our room.

"Something to do with paper milling. I don't remember exactly."

"Where?"

"In Mexico I think. He says he lives there. What's the difference? He'll tell us when he gets to know us better."

"I'm not so sure. He has so many bad memories. He's come back so many times to a country that's so forbidding to foreigners. And that business about not being able to go home."

"Maybe he doesn't want to."

"He said he can't. What would keep you from going home to your own country?"

"Because he'd get thrown in jail I suppose you're going to say. You get the craziest ideas. He's too charming for something like that."

"He's charming for sure. But not very easy to understand."

They sit attentively while Márgara continues her story, Camila with a wry smile, David hanging on her every word:

"My source doesn't offer up many details about Camila's life before she met Francisco. Belén and Desiderio Fuentes were alternately strict and indulgent with their offspring. Rather it would be fairer to say her mother was strict and her father was indulgent. Her golden eyes only had to cloud over with a few tears and the poor man was stammering with love and bewilderment. Such a catastrophe! (The eyes of all the subsequent Camilas have exerted the same power over members of the opposite sex.)

From the moment she met Francisco—and meeting really is such an inadequate term to describe that ephemeral brush of glances—he became the object of her desire. The first thing she did the next day was seek out more details about the family. She found out they had three sons (no daughters) who lived on the family hacienda most of the time, but that one of the boys was studying in Mexico City. And Francisco? No one knew what he did for a living. It was as though he were adopted. So she went back to Lucía: you know them, she said. Take me, take me please the next time you go. Such a step obviously required more than a little time and diplomacy. The logical connection was Lucía's friend, Luis' fiancée, but Belén wasn't persuaded. Such a young girl! And with no experience! On the other hand, it was about time she met some young men from good families. The girl would need at least some exposure before a suitable candidate could emerge to ask for her hand. That candidate was even now coming into view, however distantly on the horizon: a being of mythical virtues: family, money, age, poise, and the maturity it would take to guide such a volatile young creature. A firm but tender hand would be needed. Belén didn't have any illusions about her daughter's sense, and sought to commend Camila's future to a man less inclined to give in to the girl's whims than Desiderio. My source points out that at that time, fifteen was much further along toward the age of decision than it is now. That fact influenced her mother's decision to grant her permission. Here you might be tempted to ask whether the course of events might have been different had her mother said no. The answer, though purely hypothetical, is no. It's always been impossible to deter any Camila from her purpose once she's set her mind to it.

"In anticipation of receiving guests, San José was adorned in all its finery. The tree-lined drive, the patios, the fountains, and the shimmering blue sky that never clouded over. It nearly made Camila forget why she had come. The day began with a breakfast that was almost too lavish: stews, tamales, glazed bread fresh from the oven, salsas of every color, so spicy they made her sneeze. The youthful guests laughed loudly around the table, ready to head out and ride. They regarded the new asset, imagining promising futures with her. Though not the prettiest, she was far and away the most joyful, the most enthusiastic. The most flirtatious? Possibly, but only because she wasn't conscious of being so. Of course her flirtation had an object, though he'd disappeared from the face of the earth. She turned out to be a bold, if unskilled, rider. She danced until she was spent. Her laughter reverberated off the ancient roofs, scaring away swallows. In the end she left behind seeds that flowered in more than one young man's imagination. It was a weekend of possibility, destined to change the future course of events.

"Camila was naïve but not stupid. She disguised her questions with genuine interest in the family. What do your brothers do? Where do they study? The inquiry branched out in whatever direction occurred to her. She had fun, there is no doubt, and at times forgot her purpose. Though not for long. Francisco had become fixed in her imagination with a firmness out of proportion to all logic. Yet given the silence that surrounded his person, she began to doubt his existence. The one time his name did come up, it was almost by accident. Yes, that's my brother's chestnut mare. She seized on the opportunity: doesn't he want to ride it? She was answered with a simple no, he's not here. Where is he, she dared once again, and thought she heard an I don't know, before the topic abruptly changed. She couldn't insist, of course. That would have been too much for the conventions of her time.

"Camila assumed the role of Penelope. Francisco, the part of Ulysses. Though since he was ignorant of the role that had been given him, he did whatever he felt like. It's a shame we don't know what he was doing at the time.

"How can such a young girl be a Penelope? Camila made her phantom Ulysses the cornerstone of her future, and so escaped the fate that Jane Austen described so well: the search for a husband. Since he already existed, she was able to turn her gaze back upon herself and simply enjoy her time, in a way we can't imagine now. It must have been a wonderful time of independent pursuits: music, painting, with no ambition other than showing off at social event, or maybe for the family. We do know that Camila was a great fan of gardening. She liked to dance, and developed a real love for the countryside. And horses (perhaps in honor of the famous chestnut that she never rode). And also, strangely, of the bow and arrow. She was following in the footsteps of her mythical model, rejecting suitors continually, incomprehensibly. In sharp contrast to her descendant, my sister, she learned to say no to all her boyfriends—or boyfriends-to-be. Deep down the logic behind both attitudes may be the same. The negative Camila said no to everyone who wasn't her one original Francisco. The positive one says yes to all his possible embodiments. What they have in common is an ideal of a Francisco, one who was and is a chimera. One day she cornered Lucía and, when no one was listening, confessed her love for the absent poet. Her friend paled. Forget him, she said. You couldn't have made a worse choice. Please listen to me."

"It's my turn now," Camila interrupted. "I'm in charge of Lucía's voice, and she's a special character. That time of 'wonderful independent pursuits' never actually happened. Great-grandma couldn't even sew two stitches in row, and her idea of knitting was tangling a thread around two needles for as long as it took to make a crooked rag. Just like my sister, she always kept all her men guessing, because she could never make up her mind. But getting back to the story, what was Francisco Videgaray's awful secret? Whispering, and begging great-grandma to never, ever tell anyone who told it to her, Lucía actually started gossiping about him a little. Francisco was run out of his house, she whispered. How? Why? Well, his father ordered him to, before he dishonored his family. He's got a problem. You mean he's going to die? No silly, he's not sick, a gambling problem. Great-grandma sighed with relief. That's all? But my God, imagine the kinds of places he goes! The low-lifes he probably gets mixed up with! And on top of that—and here great-grandma had to come in close to hear her—they say he cheats. That's why he always wins. Well then he'll be rich, right? was all that Camila could think to say.

Since Lucía doesn't talk much, my stories are always shorter. It's your turn now David."

"Okay, but you'll have to wait a bit. I have a surprise for you, but I need time to get into my character. Let's take a break and I promise to start tomorrow."

Banteay Srei

The road to Banteay Srei is longer. All tourists must request permission for entry at a guard station, and pass through a small town. On the way there Márgara feels annoyed with David and herself, too. With him, for surrounding himself with a veil of mystery. Lies maybe? With herself for judging him that way, perhaps unfairly. Can't he be the respectable head of a paper concern and travel to remote countries? He must be an executive to treat matters of money with such indifference. He lives in a luxury hotel, has his own jeep—or a permanent lease, what's the difference?—and insists on picking up the check despite all protests. You can't accuse him of being a Don Juan, making dual investments in the future. No one commits himself to two immediate, simultaneous futures, as he would have to do in this case. He hasn't discussed returning to his job, nor the slightest concern for a company he abandoned who knows where. Dollars gush from his wallet as from an inexhaustible fountain. Is he some kind of heir? One who can't return to Mexico? To New York, where he says he lived for so many years? Possibly he prefers to linger in his Asian hideaway. His memories of a Cambodia that she thought was inaccessible are strange to her. But really, why should she care? He's a chance acquaintance who will disappear from their lives the moment they return to Frankfurt, or wherever her brother-in-law decides they should go to meet him. So, if he's being pursued by the law, if his love for this country is a put-on, if the money he spends so casually is ill-gotten, what does it matter to her?

You're the problem, Márgara, you can't accept the idea that life, or people, can be one-dimensional. Even as a girl you wanted to see serpents where there were only earthworms. African jungles in the flowerpots. Phantoms in every corner. Every night before you went to sleep you lived like a protagonist in one of your books. But now you've grown, Márgara, Margarita. You can't even accept your own name. You want the Khmer Rouge to kidnap you, for David to be some adventurer, to enter the friezes and fight with Hanuman, to be chased by the elephants that the king hunts. Anything but to be driven from place to place in a comfortable jeep, an attentive man at the wheel, visiting temples that have been restored and swept clean.

Banteay Srei is for all intents and purposes restored. It protrudes from its leafy setting like a jewel. A miniature fairy tale in pink stone. Perfect as it is, it's hard to believe it's so much older than the rest. It seems inhabited, as if the people who dwelt there have gone for a walk and might return at any moment. They call it the Citadel of Women because of its delicate decorations and the innumerable female figures in the friezes. Camila falls in love. There are no ghosts here, she says, only beautiful memories.

"André Malraux came here with an expedition as a young man," says David. "He dove in right away, stealing sculptures and architectural details," he explains as we contemplate Banteay Srei once again, this time in a book he'd given us as we sat down to dinner.

"What would Malraux have been like at twenty-two? Probably obsessed with the Orient and with art. So much so that when he came upon some ruins that had been lost to the Western world, he wanted to take some of them back with him, something for him alone. Half-broken sculptures, friezes that had pulled away from the walls. The rationale probably came later. At the time probably all he and his team saw were objects of value for the Parisian galleries. I'd just as soon believe the story Malraux told and feign ignorance of the facts."

"They arrested him in Phnom Penh and forced him to return what he'd taken. Incredible. Especially when you read his books about art."

"If you'd discovered a place like that, that no one had ever even heard of, and you almost felt like you owned it— having found it—wouldn't you be tempted to take some of it home with you?"

"I don't know, Camila. I don't think so, but not for ethical reasons. When you fall in love with something, you don't want to see it mutilated. You want to preserve it the way it is."

"But if something fascinated you, wouldn't you want to keep it? So you can have it close to you every day of your life? I know I would."

"The Buddha and I have already conferred on that point," I tell her. "So like Malraux, you'd be capable of 'removing', to put it delicately, one of these stone women from her niche and putting her next to your door."

"What about you?" David asks me. "Would you take away an *aspara* so it could dance in your garden at night?"

"I think not. Maybe if I were to see it in an antique store, like Camila's Buddha. Someone else would have stolen it, so I could share the blame. At any rate I prefer her in her place of origin. That way I'm not responsible for her."

"In other words Camila wants to own things and Márgara doesn't want to have to be responsible for them."

This duality between contemplating and possessing is strange. I don't want to own a Buddha, nor a frieze, nor a person. Here the ruins watch me from afar and I'm insignificant. Is it what we modern pilgrims seek? The sensation that we don't matter, that nothing we do has any historical significance? The big events march forward and our little motions accommodate them. Put up against these faces of impassive stone, my time is infinitesimal. Thary doesn't think that way. And nothing that I've done or failed to do has changed that attitude. It makes me jealous to hear those two talk about the psychology of possession, to hear them recount a past they know so well they could have lived it.

The routine has been established: a nice warm bath, dinner, and Márgara slips into her storytelling persona.

"Lucía did eventually get excited about the idea of true love, when she finally stared it in the face. And where did that perfect passion come from? Books of course, the prohibited kind, which the two of them read secretly behind the big armchair in the library. Besides being intelligent, Desiderio was a liberal man, and he knew that prohibiting a vice was the same thing as encouraging it. So while he did acquire books of questionable content, he put them in hard-to-reach places, and trusted in his daughter's inherent laziness when it came to reading anything in French. On the lower shelves texts on history and philosophy could be found, as well as his extensive medical library. Novels of an edifying or moralist sort he left scattered about, apparently casually, and Camila regarded them thusly, since for her reading was an activity to be undertaken only in times of duress. Lucía's arrival altered this peaceful status quo. From the moment she first set foot in the library her eyes sparkled. She immediately cornered poor Desiderio, peppering him with questions about Latin titles, oversized volumes on Anatomy (which he resolutely declared off-limits) and travelogues. Oh, do give me permission to read some of your books, she pleaded. Desiderio was conquered, as it was a passion unknown in his family. I don't know, perhaps if you knew French. . . . Oh, I read French very well, Lucía answered. How different from his daughter! After three tutors all she was capable of were a few mumbled expressions which she delivered with a pitiable accent and even worse syntax. What a good influence this girl might be, if her enthusiasm could be channeled in the right direction. Desiderio raised his cane, outlining borders in the air. From the third to the fourth bookcases, from the red volume to the end, that is what you may read. His collection of *Romans Populaires Illustrés* resided there, serialized novels he had lovingly collected and pasted together. He had only vague recollections of the rest of the shelves' contents, but titles like *The Red Rover* by Fenimore Cooper and some Dickens novels seemed inoffensive enough. Sufficient, anyway, to distract them from trivialities like dances and hairstyles.

Camila would have preferred to spend her afternoons dreaming about The Absent One, imagining his poetical hand upon the page (she thought of his hand because his face had the frustrating habit of disappearing or blending into others) and the loving look with which he would offer her that same page, one filled with the most delightful sonnets. If only she had been able to share those illusions with some kindred spirit, her joy would have been complete. Unfortunately that spirit wasn't quite there. Lucía had no intention of becoming a repository of such interminable fantasies. Even so, Camila was her passport to Elysium. What she needed was a way to interest her friend in the stories she herself was dying to read. Once again here, my source questions the role that chance plays in individual lives. Camila was just a girl, and without the encouragement that Lucía's readings provided, Francisco might have been relegated to her trunk of lost toys.

Perched upon the library's wooden ladder, they pored over the long row of red-spined books (much larger than your usual books) and picked one. On the first page was an engraving of damsels dressed in light, airy garments frolicking among flowers. *20 centimes la livraison*. What does that mean? That it cost twenty centimes? How much is that? On the last page, in Desiderio's precise and elegant hand, the contents were listed. Novels, poems, the fables of Lafontaine, a few plays. Let's read a novel, Lucía proposed. Camila considered the number of pages involved with horror. Still, the illustration of a girl asleep on a bench while a boy gazed upon her enticed her. Thus they launched into *Valentine* with nary another thought. It was a Napoleonic serial filled with abductions, betrayals and unrequited love. And so, what at first seemed to be a Sisyphean labor became easier and easier. Long forgotten words suddenly made sense, and her eagerness to know the outcomes of so many disgraceful acts spurred her comprehension. The book was no *Madame Bovary*, yet as a result of it Camila's imagination reached new heights. Her infatuation with Francisco was naïve, but the book's romanticism transformed him into a potential lover, and her faint recollections of exchanged glances and bad poetry were transmuted into stolen kisses in the moonlight."

"That's the official version anyway," Camila continued. "But it's not what really happened. Everything would have been fine if the guy who edited *Romans Populaires Illustrés*—I can just see him in some stupid little office under a pile of books, plotting the destruction of women—hadn't put some stories by Boccaccio in the book. To this day no one knows why he decided to do what he did instead of doing his job, publishing wholesome books for wholesome families. But then we also don't know whether or not his version of Boccaccio was the real one or some Disney-fied version. That actual book, *Romans Illustrés,* got lost when they moved, so we really don't know. But the result of it all was that Belén came into the library and found them all worked up, giggling with noses stuck in that big red book. She ran off and told her husband that the girls were reading something scandalous. Of course if she'd bothered to actually look at the book she would have had a heart attack. Can you imagine what Belén would have said about a story where a woman gets carried off by a pirate (Pagamin de Monegue was his name) and then later proclaims to her husband: Pagamin is a real man! He's the husband I always wanted! He holds me in his arms all night long! He hugs me! He bites me! He caresses my body a hundred different ways! Now you tell me why I'd ever want you back! Belén happened to come in right at the moment when the two of them were puzzling over the word 'bites', which when applied to a man and a woman in a bed, instead of to a dog, made for one heck of an image. Anyway, they never noticed Belén, but when they smelled Desiderio's cigar they jumped and the book fell on the floor. The fact that it fell saved them for the moment. Lucía picked up the book and innocently opened it to a story by Lafontaine. Desiderio was suspicious though. He took the book, leafed through it, and noticed that besides Lafontaine's fables were stories by Boccaccio and from *One Thousand and One Nights,* so he confiscated it. Forever. Camila and Lucía never found out what happened to Pagamin the pirate, or what the biting was all about, but by then they knew that more than a little fun could be found in his library. It wasn't just the romance that attracted them, but the sensuality of it all. All because of that one little phrase, 'he bites me'. Just imagine it."

"As I said on that first night: what imagination, or rather memory, you two have," David interrupts. "Did you make up the story about the pirate or are you quoting word-for-word?"

The two of them laugh and look at each other complicitly. "We know it by heart," Márgara says.

"We learned it together, hiding behind the sofa at home. After that were *Lady Chatterly's Lover* and *Fanny Hill,*" Camila added.

"All because we wanted to be mysterious. We could have read it all in the light of day, and no one would have stopped us. But it was more fun that way."

"There's a lot to envy in that sisterly relationship."

"Do you and your brother get along well?"

"So much so that he's the one who makes it possible for me to be here. But I spent my youth at a boarding school in the United States, so we only saw each other during vacations. But go on, please, I didn't mean to interrupt."

"About that time Pablo Videgaray appeared on the scene. An aunt presented him like some sort of trophy. You don't find men like him around anymore (my source wondered if there really haven't been any like him since): hard-working, respectful, Christian. Who knows which of those qualities Camila disliked the most. At first she accepted him, hoping to learn more about Francisco. What better source could there be than his brother? Pablo was flattered by her interest in his family, and bragged about their stability and class, until he got bored of the topic and proposed! Well, Camila took it as an insult, like he'd asked her to have an affair. He was dumbfounded. How dare you! That shook his self-esteem a bit. From then on he never looked at himself the same way in the mirror. Belén sobbed while Desiderio smoked like mad faced with such stupidity. She's a little girl and already they want to marry her off!

Lucía was more pragmatic. Though when she insinuated that one brother was as good as another, she nearly ruined their friendship. Camila declared a moratorium on the entire suitor idea, which held for years. At first, likely candidates were everywhere, since a woman who doesn't seem to want to get married is a novelty and a challenge. In time though, rumors started circulating about strange diseases, or that she wanted to be a nun and her parents wouldn't let her. Any excuse a man would use to save face after being told to go to hell. Pablo Videgaray recovered in time to find a woman who appreciated him. Camila even went to that wedding, dressed to the nines, certain her Francisco would finally return. But it was not to be, the Earth had swallowed him up. One time, frustrated by so much pressure to get married, she invoked his name like one might a ghost. Which happened to be exactly what her parents thought he was. They didn't even remember him. A huge scene ensued, full of weeping, wailing and recrimination, though Camila endured it, secure in the knowledge that Francisco was somewhere out there, with her image fixed in his memory and heart, and that he would come back for her at the appointed time. On the day Lucía dared to ask 'And if he doesn't remember you anymore?' she frantically waved the wrinkled, faded wedding invitation in her face and threatened never to speak to her again. Camila became 'Penelope' as you say, though she wouldn't have had any idea what that meant, while she waited for her Ulysses to get tired of wandering the universe.

Ta Prohm

There is no one but us in the silence. David busies himself with studying the reliefs, and we wander without tiring. It took centuries of neglect to get to this point, with the enormous roots of the banyan and ceiba trees digging in, creating a fusion of trunk and stone. *Ta Prohm is the mirage made real from all the magical tales of cities lost in the jungle . . .* The trees grow among the walls, where they've built a second roof of green over the original one. The roots work according to their own aesthetic, redefining outlines and inventing an alternative architecture. No one can separate the temple from the jungle anymore. The destruction of one would lead to the annihilation of the other. In their age-old battle, the two adversaries have declared a truce. They now remain motionless. Joined. With no way out.

David takes a piece of paper from his wallet and gives it to me:

"What of the city?" asked the White Cobra. What of the great, the walled city—the city of a hundred elephants and twenty thousand horses, and cattle past counting -- the city of the King of Twenty Kings?" I read aloud, and remember: Mowgli.

"Good memory. The first time I came here I spent days trying to remember that sentence. It floated around in my brain and I desperately tried to place it. It's the perfect description of this place. Much later, when I reread *The*

Jungle Book, I found it. I carry it with me now so I won't lose it again.

"The great city, the walled city . . . I can imagine that old white cobra, blind, full of vengeance, watching over the treasures of the King of Twenty Kings."

"They must certainly be there among the stones. Cobras, I mean."

"It's possible. Maybe treasures too."

Márgara watches David take the paper, fold it and put it back in his wallet. The brush of his fingers makes her faintly uneasy. Maybe it's the way his eyes fix upon her for those few seconds. Some shared memory, one that must come from way back, from a childhood spent lost in the images words make, produces a momentary emotion. In the way that certain landscapes, turbulent seas or mountains disappearing into the distance tighten the throat and cause frivolous tears to fall.

"You can always bring your fantasies to life. Everything that can exist must exist somewhere. Books do no more than foretell events. The things you read create visions that wait to be discovered. You've only to follow that initial thread and have faith . . ." he says, staring at her again.

A spark of alarm appears in Camila's eyes as she senses a complicity beginning between David and her sister, one spun from affinities that she doesn't share. The spell of these places affects her too, wrapping her in a web of new sensations. But there is not, either between her and Márgara, or between her and David, that feeling that they belong to the same world. They speak from time to time, though increasingly often, in some private language of memories, alluding to parallel experiences of the imagination. Camila thinks of Bobby and wants to miss him. Would he like being here? Her husband is an urban being. He loves noise and the tumult of the city. So does she. Yet here she is being dragged along on one of Márgara's magical adventures. She's even grateful that Márgara thought to bring them here. Without you I wouldn't have seen all this. Without you where would I be? She takes David by the hand and leads him toward the great doorway, somehow held in place by roots that have taken the place of much of the stonework. A picture of the two of us, Márgara. David puts his arm around her shoulders, and she feels his shirt sleeve brush her face. Márgara focuses. She moves back, then closer, in search of the perfect angle. David pulls away, takes the camera, puts it on a broken pillar, and the two of them join her. That's better, the three pilgrims, he says, then steps between them to wait for the click.

It's hard to leave Ta Prohm. It isn't a place, it's an idea. I don't think I can ever capture all that's happened here. What David said moved me, as if I'd been transported to a world I only knew from dreams, one that I can't experience in real life. As if today weren't really real, and the moment I took my first step outside, into the jeep, everything melted away. We can come back some other day, David tells me. But I don't know if I want to come back; to run the risk of spoiling my first impression. I'd already seen images of Angkor: the faces, the reliefs. I found something more when I came here, so elusive perhaps it should be left alone.

When I drew away to take the picture that ended up being of all three of us, I was struck to see the two of them framed by the lens: what an attractive pair. Camila gazing up with that look of hers, and David, much taller, hugging her. It was only for an instant, since he pulled away immediately to come and get me. "This girl is just like my mother," Grandma Susan insisted before Camila got married, "always chasing the wrong man. Then there's Márgara. . . ." I'm grateful she never got the chance to finish that sentence. I don't resemble Camila, this one or any of the others. I'm taller and more angular, with redundant coloring: brown eyes with brown hair instead of green with ash-blonde. The fact that I'm not surrounded by men isn't due to any lack of admirers, but the fact that I'm stubbornly pursuing the perfect one (the failure of the magazine, which my brother-in-law tried to make up for with this trip, coincided with the failure of my relationship with Arturo, and happened just as fast).

The differences were utterly lost on our parents. If Camila brought home an unemployed magician and I a mute Norwegian, the reaction was the same: what a nice young man, even if he were a troglodyte. On meeting Bobby my mother remarked, "He's a romantic man from a lost breed," and moved on to the wedding without further ado. Bobby glossed over the gaps in his background with flowers and bottles of wine. Only Grandma Susan wrinkled her nose the day she met him and whispered under her breath: "same as all the others." Later Bobby won her over with hothouse violets and anise-flavored candies. He tried to win me over by arranging a long series of dates with his friends. I dined, danced, went to the theater, and rejected them one by one, until Bobby finally wrote me off as a lost cause. Grandma Susan was a lost cause in a different way. Grandpa Dante died in the Spanish Civil War and left her a widow at a young age. Family legend had it that he died a hero, though exactly what that 'heroism' entailed was never quite established. No one ever understood why he left, why he never sent word of himself, or how it was he disappeared. I suppose that isn't so strange considering a million died, and it's possible he's buried in some Republican cemetery, having fought and died bravely.

On the other hand it may be that he's eating chorizo and whiling away his days in the company of a sensuous gypsy girl, though we prefer not to tell grandma that. Our family produces more cynics than heroes. Before he disappeared Grandpa Dante acquired a reputation for eccentricity (an eccentricity that lives on in my mother's name: Minerva) as well as for his poetic skills and good looks. In his wedding photo he appears as a blonde Apollo, just like the Camilas, his mother and my sister, standing alongside his plain little wife, pale as though she'd just won the lottery. His brief appearance in Grandma Susan's life caused enough chaos to convince her that the lottery wasn't all it was cracked up to be. And thus she settled into widowhood with a certain optimism, in a comfort she owed to her family, since her husband left her in poverty. Once, when I asked her why she never remarried her response was unequivocal: one is enough, my child. The men in this family are so ephemeral that one is tempted to doubt their existence, and cultivate a belief in spontaneous generation. My father is the sole exception: his good sense reigns in the whimsy that my mother inherited along with her name, though there's certainly nothing of the heroic goddess Minerva in her. She skipped a few centuries and settled straight into Romanticism. I prefer to define myself instead of vacillating between father's groundedness and mother's adventurous yearnings. Though I suppose genes have their reasons that reason can't grasp. . .

"My turn tonight," David says. "My surprise is I'm going to tell Francisco's story. Since neither one of you knows it, who's to say I'm wrong? You'll see . . .

"Francisco Videgaray lived the myth of the Old West before it even existed. My source (and he's completely trustworthy) told *me* that the idea we have of the West is a myth, created in our collective imagination by books and especially movies. Thus at the end of the 19th century the Old West was still a real place, with all the familiar figures, but it hadn't taken its place in the geography of fantasy. Heroes abounded, and their deeds, astonishing as they were, were remembered. But the legend was still in the making. The cowboys, the pioneers, the gold-miners, the gunslingers, bad guys maybe, if it isn't too politically incorrect to say so, the homesteaders and their mad wagon races to stake out the best plot of land, the Indians (who've since been transformed by our changing ideologies from assassins to victims), the entire cast of that archetypal movie we know as the American West was in place, but it was all too close to be appreciated as the fiction it would become.

"Francisco Videgaray didn't match any of those archetypes. He didn't have any intention of being a pioneer, working the land from sunup to sundown while his woman's skin turned to leather and her imagination wafted away like so many wisps of smoke over the lye cauldron or the cooking fire, with Indians crouched nearby, waiting for a chance to scalp them. He was an aristocrat, a landowner by birth, and the hired hands on his Porfirian hacienda swung hoes while their women cooked and washed the clothes. He had beautiful horses that he'd trot around the countryside, and would never have dreamt of using them for a cattle drive. He knew how to shoot, and hunted well enough, but had never stared down the wrong end of a hogleg. As far as gold was concerned, it was something his father kept in chests after it had been minted into coins. The Indians, the redskins, were a complete unknown. All in all, not the stuff that movies are made of. What motivated him then, to leave behind his many comforts and venture off into unknown territory? My source tells me he was a restless kid, the kind who gets bored easily (we saw that in the wedding scene at the beginning of the story), who has precious little appreciation for the tranquility and privilege of his childhood home. Someone always has a sob story to tell about a cruel or dictatorial father or a sanctimonious, manipulative mother. He didn't have either one, so we can't label him a victim. Fausto Videgaray was a quiet man whose perseverance eventually amassed him a fortune. Edelmira was a dependable wife and mother, more good-natured than strict. You wouldn't find murderous jealousy, incestuous temptation, or resentment in that house. In truth, when Francisco left, the family actually missed him, thought of him every day, and stood ready to welcome him with open arms when he felt like coming back. No one called him a prodigal son or plotted to steal his inheritance. In other words, no movie plot material there either.

People, being what they are, rebel against all sorts of things: social injustice, political dictatorship, intolerance, repression. Others believe their lot in life has very little to offer. They've got no idea what they want, but they sense that it must be better than what they have. These people become travelers, to find the thing they imagine, or artists, to create what they seek: they paint, they compose, they write or sing, as if some perfect note will suddenly bring the thing that they desire to life in all its splendor. Francisco simply decided that his life lacked stimulation and he'd have to find it elsewhere. The gambling habit helped a bit. Fausto, being neither dictatorial nor cruel, was at first simply bothered at the notion of paying his son's debts. Later he was bothered that there were no more debts to pay, only profits, profits tinged by rumor (vague of course, because the Videgarays were respected members of the community). Francisco justified his earning by citing his innate ability with cards (which was indisputable), and uncanny luck (slightly implausible). His brothers backed him up on both counts. No one could prove foul play, yet whenever any unwary soul, be they family, friend or acquaintance, found their way to his gaming table they were summarily fleeced. Finally, when his recklessness and wastefulness became conspicuous, Fausto decided Francisco was dealing with his family's honor as well as with cards. He demanded an end to all activities related to gaming: cards, dice, roulette. Everything, in short, that was governed by the laws of chance (or that special brand of chance that comes of a single individual's making). Francisco acceded to his father's wishes without complaint (it isn't clear if it was out of obedience, affection or the simple deduction that his well of suckers was running dry). He was offered alternatives: to take over the administration of the hacienda, for example, to continue his studies in the capital or abroad, to get married.

This is how he came to be at the wedding. Edelmira dragged him there. Francisco knew what she was up to of course, and to him Camila was dangerous. Generically dangerous, in the way that any pretty girl could be, especially if they were so easily impressed by his poetic flights of fancy. He went home that night determined to find new pastures where his liberty would be preserved.

"The story Lucia told Camila, that Francisco was run off the family estate, never happened. Or so my source tells me. It wasn't a dramatic episode. Rather Francisco simply announced one day that he needed time to consider his future, and so had decided to travel. His father had his doubts about his motivations. His mother secretly wept. His brothers watched in admiration as he packed a suitcase suspiciously lacking in formal attire. The farewell was warm and affectionate.

"The character of Francisco is rather blurry up until this point in the story. It's blurry to us, and was blurry to him as well. His most serious problem, or perhaps it was a virtue, was a lack of ambition. The only thing he liked to do was play: play with figures, play with numbers, play with words. This is where his fondness for poetry and cards came from (and of course he was more successful in the latter). The attraction that sparked between Francisco and Camila was probably born of similar temperaments, as well as their mutual dissatisfaction with the ordinary. Since my source is a man, and as such not very interested in how character traits play themselves out differently in the lives of the sexes, he doesn't spend much time on them. The age, on the other hand, was very sensitive to the ways these things worked. Had Francisco been a woman he might have become a poet, or a painter, the type who stows her work away in the attic for lack of opportunity to show it. If Camila had been a man she might have hopped a train North to find a new life. But under the circumstances, Camila was the one who stayed at home reading *Romans Illustrés,* pining, while Francisco took the train. Both had their ways of showing their restless nature. . . ."

Márgara is moved. Somehow right there in David's voice, was the phantom whose destiny had been lost to family memory. Or, for propriety's sake, was hidden from view.

"Your portrait of the family is awfully romantic, David," Camila says. "Only there wasn't that idyllic harmony you mentioned. Francisco was a disaster, really. Ever since he was a boy he spent all his time with farm hands, and eventually some lowlife took him under his wing: Nacho the Rooster whose nickname pretty much says it all. He and Nacho trained a fighting cock and one night the three of them, Nacho, Francisco and the rooster, took off to the pit. Well, it goes without saying that the bird was so vicious that pretty soon Nacho was a wealthy man, and Francisco found himself wishing he had money of his own to put down. I guess it's because people didn't leave their wallets lying around at that time, or because children didn't receive allowances, but Francisco resorted to extreme measures: he pilfered some coins from Refugio the cook, claiming it was 'a loan'. That was all the seed money he needed to start his career as a gambler. The bird continued his winning streak and soon another younger one was added to the lineup. Everything would have been peachy if it hadn't been for a sudden generous impulse, though his family never believed it. As soon as he won his first bet, he ran off to make good on the loan. Noticing the ridiculous sum in his hand, he decided it was only fair to make Refugio a partner in the wager she had unwittingly financed. Refugio simply assumed that some mystical force was working on her behalf. And so, in the hope of not missing out on any more good fortune, she increased the quantity and variety of saints on her altar and the novenas she dedicated to each one. But then one day she found out which saint was working for her, walking on tiptoes and sneaking money into the knotted handkerchief she had hidden behind the kitchen stove. Simple soul that she was, Refugio cried out. Francisco froze. And of course Doña Edelmira chose that very moment to walk through the kitchen door. So there they are: a horrified mother, a pleading cook, and a terrified son telling impossible tales. Your idea that Edelmira was, how did you put it, David? "more good-natured than rigid" is plain wishful thinking. She picked him up by the hair and shook him until he confessed where he'd gotten the money. Francisco, stricken at the prospect of meeting the big boss, his 'good man' father, squealed like a stuck pig 'It's mine! I won it!' It went from bad, to worse. 'You won it, doing what?' And then he spilled it: the rooster, the pit, the betting. Though to his credit he never mentioned Nacho. And so it seemed to everyone that he was a self-made delinquent, without any accomplice to share the blame. Edelmira was so furious that she didn't even think to call Fausto. But she did call to the stand the accessory to the crime: the rooster, who was directly hauled to the kitchen, crying in fury. The 'good-natured' mother promptly grabbed the rooster by its feet, swung him like a two-handed sword and brought him down with a thud on Francisco's head. Francisco let out a howl, dropped to the floor and slunk away, hiding himself behind Refugio's skirt. The rooster was killed in the encounter, possibly at the moment of impact or as a consequence of wounds received. When Fausto finally heard the story he fell silent, either fuming over his son's exploits or marveling at his wife's temper. The upside for Francisco was that in all the excitement no one remembered to confiscate the money, which became the stake for his future business dealings. After the fact, when people called him egotistical and scatterbrained, they had no idea that his first and only generous impulse died with that chicken, in one ferocious whack on the head."

Angkor Wat

The **fog lifts**, but with difficulty. From within its midst, platforms appear, staircases, and farther away, almost out of view, the towers. Light melds the buildings into an enigmatic whole. We walk slowly, circling the wall, over and over, our gaze fixed on the summit, the sunless sky turning from gray to white. We hesitate to enter and begin our ascent. It would feel like trespassing. An intrusion into the silence. A challenge to the sacred thing we sense in the interior. As if our footsteps, each in their turn, trampled the time that had accumulated on the stairs. Who was the first modern soul who dared to push aside the undergrowth and venture into the domain of the Khmer colossus?

No one else is here at this hour. David made a date with us for six, then drove us in silence the few kilometers to the western entrance. He let us walk ahead, not wanting to introduce a human element to the panorama in front of us, tiny though it would have seemed. Angkor opens again and again before a visitor, hiding each part of itself, offering up surprises where you'd think no more would fit. From the entrance I see the causeway with its guardian lions and moat: a mirror the light has yet to awaken. Then at last, the silhouette of the towers: deep gray masses against the sky's white timidity, mute witnesses of something that's vanished from our time but is alive in another. Like faithful pilgrims of old, we cross the entrance pavilion and approach the temple with its cross-shaped cloisters and vaulted galleries on whose walls the whole history of this vanished civilization is written. One by one we visit the pyramidal terraces. From the highest one I can see the others below me, and the line of the causeway disappearing over the horizon.

What can you say about Angkor Wat? It defies all attempts to capture it in words. Its space, its volume, its perfect galleries and bas-reliefs, its places of worship. All combine to create a monument on a scale that human strength alone could never achieve, which is why the Khmers attribute it to the divine architect, Visvakarman. Little by little the sun reveals the outlines, the pinnacle of the central tower with its crown of lotus blossoms. Little by little it fills with people, though for us the day stands still. We spend hours trying to interpret the history being told in the bas-reliefs: battles, love affairs, benevolent (or vengeful) gods, horses agonizing beneath the enemy's spear. *The whole epic of India, grafted onto the Khmer imagination, lives on here in stone,* shielded from the sun and rain so that the deeds of its heroes might be eternally repeated.

David takes me by the arm:

"I'm starving. I need a good whisky and an easy chair."

"So soon?"

"We got here at six thirty, we've been here for hours. What's 'soon' about that?"

"But there's so much left."

"If you want to follow the whole Hindu mythology step by step, it'll take days. We'll come back tomorrow."

The inscriptions speak of 39 kings in the Angkor period. One of the most powerful, Suryavarman III, built the temple at Angkor Wat. His ambassadors reached as far as China and his empire to the dawn of the Middle Ages, his jungles bristling with towers. You can see his royal figure in the bas-reliefs of the south gallery, astride an elephant, reviewing his troops. The endless friezes don't just teach mythology and history. Everyday life has its place here. In one panel fields are being planted, the clothing so similar to the *sampots*, those rectangles of cloth that men wear like pants and women tie at their waists like long skirts. The ancient versions were made of embroidered silk, interwoven with gold from China. Today they're cotton, dyed in sober colors for the men and joyful ones for the women. We see them as we're leaving, citizens of Campuchea visiting the vestiges of their former splendor. They wear the same clothes as the others, who remain frozen in their stony night. They have the same facial features, the women are just as elegant. Only the name Khmer is different, having been changed into something sinister when before it was glorious.

From the jeep we get a last glimpse of the gate. The outside walls give no clue as to what's hidden within. It has been a silent excursion. When I heard David's voice clamoring for whisky, it came from far away, as if from a person who had only just regained the ability to speak. We don't speak the entire way home. Maybe we really do need the whisky, or at least a little time, to recover a sense of the present.

"Thank you, David," Camila says, finally.

"Why?"

"For being such a terrific guide. And for leaving Angkor Wat until the end."

"And for your patience," I say. "For taking another trip to a place you know so well."

"I never pass up an opportunity to go to Angkor. It's not about the number of trips you take. You could see it a thousand times and never really know it. 'Its magic will go with you wherever fate and the gods may take you to color your thoughts and dreams to life's very end.'"

"I had no idea you had this poetic side."

"Oh that quote isn't mine I'm sorry to say. Some English traveler wrote it, I don't remember who. Call it shameless plagiarism, but then I think you knew that. I borrowed it because I think it expresses a feeling you'll come to understand in time."

It's every bit as beautiful in peacetime. Nowadays you're free to wander, and without fear of any unwelcome surprises. I had Thary with me that night, and an armed guard. There was a different silence then. Now it's serene. Then it was ominous, as though there was something lying in wait behind the walls. At times we could hear the bombs like distant thunder. Thary trembled with every blast, her grip on my hand becoming ever tighter. Even so she managed to forget it and let herself be spellbound. It was the most beautiful night, with no moon to blot out the stars. Only there, on the horizon, those glints of red. And later the murmur of the falling stones and water cascading into the river. The last in a short series of moments that were ours.

Márgara watches him juggle his much longed-for whisky and his pipe, which he struggles to light. It's a repeating act that inserts a few moments of silence into our conversation. He has strong hands, too strong for a pianist, even an amateur. Whose hands are they? An engineer's, perhaps? Someone who doesn't mind swapping his pencil for a pick and shovel when it's required. How old-fashioned you are, Márgara? Engineers use computers and backhoes. Picks and pencils belong to prehistory. And anyway who cares? That's just how his hands are. Later she watches as they scamper up the keyboard. Yet it seems like there's no purpose to their play. They bound aimlessly from one piece to the next, merely fiddling with the chords. Still we quiet down to listen. Someone in the bar, who's evidently heard him before, asks him to sing. Tonight it's not cocktail music. His songs are from far away. From the Scottish highlands, or from Ireland perhaps. Dialects that aren't even comprehensible. Nostalgic tunes about lands and loved ones lost. Camila gets up and goes to sit beside him. Without stopping David inches to the far edge of the bench to make room for her. She watches his hands on the keyboard and looks up at him. He picks up his glass, which hasn't moved from the piano, and offers it to her. Careful to not disturb his movements, Camila draws back a bit, rests her head upon his shoulder, and closes her eyes, lulled either by the music or his nearness.

With a gesture Márgara calls the waiter over and asks for the check. This will be one time David won't get a chance to pay it. She's eager to leave them and go up to bed. From the piano bench, David sees her sign the bill, gets up and comes over.

"Getting tired of putting up with my all my wrong notes?"

"No, it's all beautiful to me. It's just that we got up so early. . . ."

"You're right. But I hope you didn't just pay the bill, especially not my part."

"You shouldn't always be taking care of us."

"I didn't think it was a problem."

"Camila will back me up on this," she says with a glance over to the piano bench, but it's empty. David casts his eyes about the bar, but he and Márgara are the only ones left besides the waiter, who's standing there regarding them.

"I guess your sister decided to abandon us. Want a brandy? It's a delectable evening. Let's take it out to the terrace and let this poor guy go to bed."

"Not tonight, thanks. It's late . . . good night."

She lingers a moment in the vestibule, then climbs the stairs to her room. She notices David speaking to the waiter, who hands him a bottle and a glass. David sits down at the piano again.

Their room is completely dark. Shutting the door she can barely discern Camila lying in her bed. Are you asleep? No answer. She tiptoes to the bathroom to avoid waking her.

Another Version of Francisco

Your turn, Márgara."

"No, you two should continue. My Camila is, uh . . . sleeping. Call her Sleeping Beauty? I've got no sense for life in those days. I can speak to events, feelings and the like, but not day-to-day life . . . what it would have been like for them to get up in the morning, have breakfast, pass the day, some sunny or rainy afternoon, a long summer night.... Our life is so much more compartmentalized. You study so you can get a job. You work so you can be successful. You make friends, play sports, go dancing, travel. I can't imagine great-grandma Camila at home. The streets of old Mexico City are as foreign to me as Baghdad, maybe even more so, since I can at least make up some mythical Baghdad. No doubt nineteenth-century Mexico is a part of my family and my history. It's documented. It exists in time but it's so far away for me, inaccessible really. As far away from me as that girl who falls in love with a chimera and settles down to wait, wait with no real hope of him ever coming back. To bring her to life in my mind I need a better idea of who Francisco was. He's like a mirror. Without a clear picture of him I can't tell Camila's story. So go on you two."

"My Francisco just left for America, and yours is only a child, Márgara," says David. "Camila, why don't you pick up with your Francisco?"

"When I left him he had quite a bit of money, a dead rooster and another one in training. But since I don't know much about cock-fighting and my source is a little sketchy on the details, I'm going to skip ahead a few years. He's still a family outcast (even though David imagines it differently), but the trainee rooster has been doing fairly well, and Francisco has been able to use the profits to move up to card playing. David's Francisco said that he liked to play, remember, and that he was lucky. The truth is he became a first-class gambler. He was handsome (all three of our Franciscos are handsome), and that doesn't hurt. He was kind, though a troubled home life gave him a cynical edge that made him an even more effective gambler. He practiced all the time, dazzling the farm hands, his friends, brothers, and the few girls who hovered around them, not exactly angels, any of them. Girls from better families would have been at home, where daddy would keep them safe from handsome gamblers, except the ones they ran into at weddings. Francisco always seemed to end up involved with unsavory characters. From Nacho the Rooster he moved on to an old drunkard, some former gambler who'd made his way to town and was hanging around with nothing to do. He was delighted to find an apprentice, an eager student to whom he could pass on the skills of his former life. He broke Francisco in pitching pennies and throwing dice in alleyways. Soon they moved up to cantinas. He admired Francisco's innate talents, much greater than his own. When he finally ran out of things to teach him, they parted ways, though not before the old swindler gave him some advice. 'Son, remember that Lady Luck always comes back to take her cut. Someday you'll cross paths with a gambler who's better than you, and he'll either beat you or show you up for the flimflammer you are. The smart man knows to get when the getting's good. Don't go trying to use what I've shown you around here. Because even though you're the boss man's son, they'll kick you right in your skinny ass.'

"Having run out of easy marks, Francisco began to play among his acquaintances, though with precautions. He left the sleight-of-hand behind and contented himself with winning fair and square, which wasn't hard. But the temptation to use his new skills was strong. At first he was so crafty no one noticed they were being duped. And anyway, no one wanted to think such a thing of a Videgaray. But then one day a rich fellow from the capital arrived with some friends looking for a game. Well it wasn't long before, out of the goodness of their hearts, the townsfolk arranged one with the local champion. Which is to say, Francisco, plus some of the other local card sharps. I don't really know the details, but I can imagine what went on. There they were, hunkered down around a table in a candlelit room (there wasn't any electricity then, or was there?), servants standing by with drinks and cigars, the women banished to their rooms so as not to disturb the play. The hands came out fairly even at first, though little by little Francisco's pile of chips began to grow. And, little by little, that city fellow's eyebrows started to rise. He began watching the cards closely. For suddenly, it seemed, here was an extra king. Or maybe an ace. Sometimes it was just an innocent three or a five, but enough to make a hand. Of course the man had to do his counting piecemeal, since no one ever gets dealt a whole deck in a single hand. But when the losses started to become unacceptable, he stared straight at Francisco and accused him: 'you're playing dirty, partner.' All fell silent, save for some murmuring. After a moment Francisco rose, gathered his cards, and calmly told him that if he didn't know how to lose he shouldn't play. This was simply more than the poor fellow could take. He leapt up, shoved the table aside, dove upon Francisco and rained blows down on him. Their friends intervened immediately, tackling one and pushing the other toward the door. The room was a riot of shouts and fisticuffs. No one knows how they managed to calm the stranger, whom they promptly sent back to wherever it was he came from. There were a few half-hearted defenses of Francisco, some conciliatory slaps on the back, don't worry about it hombre, those city dudes have no manners. Yet secretly there were doubts, compounded by those that had arisen before, but that no one wanted to pay attention to. When Fausto found out what had happened, he called Francisco's brothers to him in turn. Luis held up well, denying all that was deniable. Pablo, however, was caught unawares. He stammered, got confused, and ended up spilling everything. Yes, things were being said, but they were lies, utter lies. How could you possibly believe it, papa? Which was the moment Fausto suddenly believed everything. Francisco wisely disappeared for a while. But when in the end he was finally called to account (in a solemn session behind closed doors) he didn't bother to play innocent. Maybe he wanted to leave, or he just got tired of all the drama. He endured his father's ferocious tirade without saying a word. David would have you believe it was all loving good byes. In reality they ran him off—good riddance! Sure his mother may have shed a few tears, and his brothers, admiring his audacity, may have thrown an arm around his neck. But that was the extent of it. And so there he is, ready for the next chapter in the story."

Tonle Sap

The *naga* king couldn't have drunk up all the water in the area, since quite a bit of it can still be found in lake Tonle Sap, whose shores merge into the horizon. From its icy source in the Himalayas, the Mekong river travels down through China, Laos, and Thailand before crossing Cambodia on its way to the China sea. In Phnom Pen it's joined by the Tonle Sap River, and the confluence causes an event that Cambodians accept as routine, but which to me seems like a miracle. At the end of the monsoon season the water rises at such a rate that the Tonle Sap reverses its course, causing it to flow back into the lake of the same name. This causes the lake to swell to more than twice its usual size, covering trees and homes. When the last vestiges of the Himalayan snows disappear, the river relents, regains its composure, and resumes its normal, tranquil flow. The great lake descends, and activity returns to the shores until the next flood. Cambodians understand it. They anticipate it. The houses in the little village of Siem Reap, far from the hotel and its park, are all built on pontoons or stilts. Children and animals meander in the shade of their lofty dwellings. The magic of this country goes far beyond mere monuments and sculptures. Rivers flowing in two directions? Rice that grows four inches a day and can reach twenty feet? Floating rice and floating houses. That's how the inhabitants of the lake make their living, swaying to the rhythm of the undulating waters, in boats that line the shores. We navigate down the middle of the canal, dodging cargo launches, merchant canoes, "school buses," and tiny gardens that barely clear the water, nudged along by a grandmother's oar, her face hidden by a conical straw hat. The community's entire life is on display in front of us. A mother bathes her children on the pier, fishermen repair nets, old people squat, contemplating the passing traffic. Everything is colorful, everything is different, everything is fascinating. I can't stop taking pictures. Though I try to be discreet by using a telephoto lens, there is an urgency not to let any of this strange aquatic world escape.

Everything is color, everything is different, everything is . . . poor. How can poverty be so sad in your own country and picturesque in others? Or is it the water that transforms it?

"Does much fishing go on?" I ask.

"When the water goes down it's easy to trap the fish. You'll see the traps in the lake soon enough."

"I was thinking about those Mexican villages where the ground has turned white from drought, where the only green are those ash-colored cactuses. Here you don't feel that desperate dryness. . . ."

"Cambodia ought to be a rich country. Or fertile at any rate. War has ruined everything here—the land, the rice fields, the little farming communities—which is ironic since the war was supposed to create a rural Eden."

"What kind of crazy man pushes a country to the edge of disaster?"

"A crazy man backed by other crazy men. Look there, we're already reaching the lake."

A liquid landscape pours out in front of us. The cloud-splotched sky reflects the blue of the lake beneath it, but the surface is so still there's no distinction between them, and the fishing canoes seem suspended. Rows of perfectly vertical poles are the only things that belie the illusion: fish traps, for the schools that are deprived of deep shelter at this time of year. We advance imperceptibly until we too are suspended in the luminosity, marred only by tatters of clouds and the wakes of passing canoes.

We arrive at a kind of floating shantytown, wood houses with crooked roofs, a labyrinth of slouching piers and flotsam-covered avenues.

"They're fisheries," says David. We moor at a pier, one that's covered by rectangular pools where the creatures swim (fish or serpents?). Camila screams and grabs David's arm. "I hate, I can't stand, any animal that creeps." He leads her back to the boat and returns for me.

"Do reptiles bother you?"

"No."

We enter a small structure. A boy, practically a baby, crawls on the wooden floor. A mother cooks something on a stove. A father squats nearby, eating rice from a bowl. When the boy approaches, the father offers him his lunch. With three fingers he holds out a ball of Oriental rice, white as chalk, compact, moist. The boy laughs, not quite managing to swallow the mouthful, grasping at what's fallen against the floor with tiny hands. The mother watches unperturbed. On one of the walls there are shelves, and on them small replicas of traps, of canoes in miniature. They look like *jai alai* baskets, woven out of very fine wicker. It's a store. On the floor there's something moving: a long, thick serpent (a small boa?) moves slowly, heavily around the boy, the father, toward the woman at the stove. He grasps the serpent, rises and offers it to me. I look at David.

"Does he want us to buy it?"

"No, you're supposed to put it around your neck."

"Like a stole?"

"Exactly. Just a little gimmick for the tourists," he says with a playful spark in his eye.

"When in Rome . . ." I say as I take the snake from the man's hands and wrap it around my neck. It's beautiful, gray, and striped like a tiger. It resists me for a moment, at least until it finds a comfortable posture, its tail rising up beside me. The man puts the serpent's head in my right hand and gestures for me to hold on tight. "Does it bite?" I ask, trying to sound confident.

"This kind doesn't bite—though it could strangle you," David says in amusement.

People think of reptiles as slimy. In reality the boa is warm with dry, smooth skin, pleasant to the touch. I play with it for a while until David takes it and returns it to the man. He looks at me, grinning, and caresses my face with the back of his hand. Looks good on you.

I ask David if we should pay them something for the snake rental, he says no.

"But it's their livelihood. . . ."

"These people are very proud. Let's just buy something."

He takes off his sweater and we fill it with little baskets, toys and figurines. He pays and we head back to Camila.

History has a way of reducing civilizations to just a handful of their most basic, classical elements. The word "Athens" conjures images of the Parthenon or the theater. Egypt, the pyramids and the sphinx. The intervening ages disappear. Surviving architecture, monuments, and statues speak of myths. They ignite the imagination with their grand stories. The present is lived by individuals like us. Would the burden of all that glory be too much to carry around with them day to day? I come from a country full of footprints, but I don't consider myself their heir.

Historical ruptures make us trustees but not owners. Do the Greeks of today see themselves as heirs of Pericles or Fidias? Probably just stewards of something that can't be emulated. When David talks about Pol Pot and the madness of a return to a rural existence, he doesn't bring up the past, that of the ancient Khmers, who built these beautiful buildings. All those intervening centuries are lost. Pol Pot's Khmers only sought to recover the primitive part, the roots, without the creative splendor. Those are the Khmers we've seen today on the lake, who wash their clothes in the river and go about in canoes filled with color. I wonder what they think when they visit their temples. Most of the people that go there are from this country. Maybe Angkor seems as foreign to them as it does to us. Maybe they see it as part of a mythic time inhabited by unique and extraordinary beings. What sense do these buildings make in a land laid waste by hunger and war, where survival is what matters and art must wait for more giving times?

The Old West

For a man looking to gamble, the logical place would have been New Orleans," David begins. "Or one of the slow boats that cruise the Mississippi carrying cotton and casinos. But Francisco wasn't an expert in geography, and that saved him from falling into the hands of professional gamblers prematurely. His instincts took him north, to the land of liberty, where he could lose himself while he accumulated some experience. He intuited that it was better to travel light, so he only packed the essentials. He accepted a small sum of his father's money to complement his own savings (and in fact they were savings, despite what Camila says), and put together a tentative itinerary that called for boarding a northern train at the Buenavista station in Mexico City. He picked the closest point of entry in order to avoid areas of tribal conflict. As we've said, Francisco didn't have a very good sense of direction. To him 'north' simply constituted a vast ill-defined area. His idea of experience didn't include bloody Indian fighting. We might imagine, though my source wasn't specific, how such a long trip might have been awe-inspiring for a landscape painter, or a social scientist. But Francisco was bored to tears. We already know how easily bored he was, and so the train trip was nearly intolerable. He dozed, lulled by the murmur and sway of the car. He idly scribbled a few bad poems. At every station he got out to take a walk and stretch his legs. From time to time he allowed himself to be seduced by some of the colorful characters he met or by the fields that flew by the window. But in general his mind was a blank. Near the end he was seized by a moment of doubt. What did he hope to gain from all this? Nothing, he decided. Nothing that could be explained, anyway. So he left himself open to whatever he might find, or what might come find him.

"When he finally got off the train he was ready to get right back on again. Compared to his house on the hacienda, to say nothing of Mexico City, this dusty, ramshackle town was a disaster. His suitcase in hand, he went in search of a hotel and a bath. He needed a place where he could sit, eat and take stock of the situation. But it didn't look any prettier. The hotel was an unpainted structure with a flimsy, provisional appearance, as though it had been thrown together yesterday with the intention of knocking it down today. A scraggly fellow standing nearby grunted something unintelligible. At the same time he made some sort of sign, tilting his head back and extending his fingers in front of his face. Francisco supposed the signal was meant to indicate the price, that or the room number. Or maybe it was just some obscene gesture, in which case he chose to ignore it. The man went up the stairs ahead of him, opened a door and practically pushed him inside with his stare. Francisco set his suitcase down on the bed, glanced at himself in the old stained mirror, and started hunting around for a bathroom. In one corner was a receptacle far too small to hold a person. Beside it were a washbasin and a pitcher of water. He opted to put off the bath until he could find more suitable amenities, then went down to the area that served as a kind of all-in-one saloon/reception desk/restaurant/gaming parlor. A hush came over the room as he descended the stairs. Every eye was fixed on him. Their owners were sweaty individuals of a distinctly menacing appearance, leaning against the bar or seated around various tables. Two of them were women dripping with make-up. On some of the tables cards and money could be seen. He'd have felt like an extraterrestrial if he'd known what the word meant. He was definitely citified in appearance. His clothing and conspicuous lack of arms made him the proverbial sore thumb. He was amazed by the abundance of artillery in the room. Almost everyone was carrying a sidearm (or two) on his belt. There were shotguns propped up against the wall.

Taking the shortest path to the bar, he faced the barkeep while he pondered his order. The barkeeper made it easy for him, slapping down a bottle and a glass without saying a word. Francisco poured his own drink. His first swig all but ended his adventures on the spot. He'd never tasted such a vile liquid in his life. His throat closed, his eyes teared, and an uncontrollable nausea swept over him. The barkeep simply stared. The silence was closing in on him. I will die here, he thought. In a vain attempt to hide his malaise he coughed loudly. The barkeeper grimaced, others chuckled a bit. This will be good for my cold, he murmured hoarsely. The barkeeper leaned in within an inch of his face.

"Spanish?" he asked loudly. Francisco thought for a moment. What would be the most innocuous response? His accent would surely betray him as a foreigner.

"From Mexico," Francisco murmured.

"Oh, Spanish!" said the man. "You want to play?" he asked, gesturing to the tables.

"Oh no, I never play," Francisco said abruptly. With that Francisco ceased to be of interest to the bartender, who drew away and began talking to another customer. Francisco pondered his next move. He was dying of hunger, but trembled at the idea that the food might be comparable in quality to the drink. A gray-haired man at a nearby table took notice of him.

"Howdy, pilgrim," he said in a peculiar accent. "Sit yourself down and have a drink." Francisco made a quick appraisal of his face. He wasn't drunk and in fact seemed to have had a bath in the last few weeks. He approached him.

"Francisco Videgaray, at your service," he murmured, punctiliously. The man gestured to a chair.

"My name is Don Pedro de Guzmán," he said. "I'm a Spaniard, just like you." Francisco wondered what a man with a name like that might possibly be like.

"I'm not Spanish, I'm Mexican." He answered. The man guffawed.

"With that name and that face!" he said. "Look at yourself! *Those* are Mexicans," he said pointing to a corner where five loud fellows in sombreros were taking turns at a bottle. "You are Spanish." Francisco didn't want to start an argument.

"All right, " he said. "I'm from Mexico City."

"Well you're a long way from home, Videgaray, my boy," the man said. "What brings you to these parts?"

"That's not fair, David,"Márgara interrupts."Francisco is the black sheep of the family and you're making him out to be some sort of gentleman."

"I'm honoring your great-grandma! How could she fall in love with a varmint?"

"She didn't fall in love with the person of Francisco, it was the mirage she loved."

"What about feminine intuition?"

"That's a myth, just an excuse women use."

"I think modern women like you are as intuitive as your grandmothers, but deny it."

"I agree with you," says Camila. "And I'll prove it, if you promise to tell me the truth. I'll bet there's a skeleton in your closet and that's why you're here instead of home in Mexico."

"You're so impertinent, Camila," Márgara says .

David suddenly finds himself caught between the two sisters, one furious, the other all but daring him to speak.

"Is that intuition or a guess?" David says. "All right then, in answer to your question, I can go back to Mexico, though I can't leave this place right now. Not that I can't but because I don't want to. There's no intrigue, just a long story that's a lot less interesting than Francisco's. And on that note I'm temporarily out of ideas. So I'm afraid I'm going to have leave you here wondering what happens to him in that miserable little town."

"And wondering why it is you don't want to leave this place." Camila says.

"Why would I leave when I've got young ladies as charming as you two to keep me company?"

"Oh you're so smooth. So does that mean that if we were to leave you'd leave too?"

"Is that an invitation?"

"Well, since David's out of ideas—for his story, I mean—I'm going to bed. Are you coming, Camila?"

"I'll be there soon."

It beggars belief that Camila would say such things. How she could pry into other people's lives like that . . . try and force them to air their dirty laundry? David's always been private, and he has every right to be so. Márgara gets into bed and stares angrily into a book while she waits for Camila to come back. Oh, is she going to get it. She wakes, no telling how much later, under blinding lamp light with an empty bed beside her.

The Other Side of Angkor Wat

My **anger** doesn't last. I wanted to strangle Camila last night, but today I don't want to anymore. All I said to her was, how dare you pressure David that way? You're the one with the doubts about him, she replied, and besides it didn't bother him, he was just as charming as ever. Clearly, I answered. We finished dressing in a hostile silence.

Our nightly sessions are going later and later. We inhabit several different time periods all at once, none of them real. The time we inhabit by day isn't ours. It's that place of worn-out splendor, with a mythology that David recounts so vividly it's as though he'd lived it. Even so, he possesses none of the qualities that I typically associate with the Orient: mysticism, the quietude of philosophies that trust in a perfect cosmic order. His style—can you call it that?—from the way he chooses wine or plays the piano, to his expensive clothing, the way he all but throws money away, all contrast with his love for this culture and these stones. It's the love of an archeologist, or an historian, and it compels him to interpret it for us.

The nighttime began as a game but has transformed into a world of possibility, created in three voices. The history that Camila and I have embroidered with our imagination since we were girls has become communal property. David adopted the voice of The Absent One and gave him life. At times I suspect that somehow he already knew it, that somebody somewhere told him what we've never known.

At times, I'm struck by the unreality of our being here. I have lost count of the days. I feel as though we'll be here forever, that we have nowhere to go and no reason to leave.

We go back to Angkor Wat, at another time and in another light. The midday sun reveals different shapes, contours we hadn't seen before. The luminosity of the patios versus the shady cool of the corridors, the bright-stained images of the faithful placing flowers and candles before impassive Buddhas. It is a living temple, rescued from the past. The violent orange of Buddhist tunics stand out in the doorways. I'd rather it were deserted, like the first time we were here, when the echo of our footsteps was the only thing we heard. When we could believe we were discovering a lost world.

As we leave, we notice that the causeway is also changed. The soft drink and bandana vendors have vanished amidst long lines of people squatting by the walkway that crosses the moat. It is a receiving line of the mutilated: men, women, and children extending their hands in mute supplication. Others, lacking arms and legs, can only beg with their eyes. Camila and I are paralyzed by the horror of it. David takes us firmly by the hand and quickens our pace. We ransack our pockets and purses for coins but find only funny money, American money. We've never had to touch the local *riel.* It is impossible to give to everyone, and so agonizing to choose. David puts some bills in a bowl that an armless girl holds with her feet. She has a pretty, adolescent face and she smiles. Impossibly, she smiles. We don't understand. It's as though a giant threshing machine had come through, chewing up human beings instead of grain stalks. Or a perverse deity had set down a collection of human figures he'd never completely finished. The questions start tumbling out of us: why, what, who, how?

"The war," David says.

"But the war ended a long time ago," I say. "These children weren't even born yet."

"Land mines," he says. "Not all casualties are inflicted by soldiers and bombs."

"How do you know?" Camila asks pointedly. There's a harshness to her voice, as though he were somehow complicit.

"How can you not know?" David asks. "It's all over the news. There's a worldwide awareness campaign about land mines and the present-day victims of forgotten wars."

Of course they know it. They've read about it. They're informed people. But that kind of knowing has little to do with what they've seen today. Márgara thinks about a book she read by a Vietnam veteran, a talented young writer who found poetry in the midst of massacre. He talked about the *Bouncing Betty,* an obscenely playful name for such a deadly device. Buried, invisible, it leaps up and shreds the body of whoever steps on it. "You try to second-guess the mine. Should you put your foot to that flat rock or the clump of weed to its rear? Paddy dike or water? You wish you were Tarzan, able to swing with the vines. You try to trace the footprints of the man to your front. You give it up when he curses you for following too closely; better one man dead than two."*

The *Bouncing Betty* isn't necessarily designed to kill but rather to mutilate. Do they use the same name for it? The mine that's destroyed all these Cambodians?

"The statistics aren't reliable, but people estimate that there are hundreds of thousands of mines scattered around Cambodia. You might call it 'the war after the war.' There've been so many victims the last few years. And

* Tim O'Brien, *If I Die in a Combat Zone* (New York: Dell, 1969), 126.

not just here. On the beaches in Vietnam you still hear about people dying in explosions. The mines are American, Chinese, Russian, the same ones you find planted all over the world."

"Who's to blame for all this?"

"There's plenty to go around. Most people blame Pol Pot and the Khmer Rouge, but then there were Vietnamese, followers of Sihanouk, and god knows who else. But in the end, the mines aren't made here in Cambodia . . ."

"David, what are you doing here?" Camila blurts out. She's serious this time. There's no light, inquiring tone like before. He answers her in kind, as if in acknowledgement that the time for guessing games is over.

"I'm here to meet someone," he says. "Someone not easy to find."

That night there are no stories, or at least no entertaining ones. Great-grandma Camila is apparently still dreaming, about something that Márgara hasn't been able to visualize yet. Francisco is left out there in the Old West, hanging.

"David, I've read articles about the Khmer Rouge," Márgara says. "I've seen the pictures, but have never really stopped to think about them. You read about so many wars in so many places. . . ."

"It's a question that's obsessed me for many years. How does a country deteriorate to the point that it becomes vulnerable to someone like Pol Pot? There are tyrants and dictators everywhere, all of them claiming there's good reason for what they do. Some people applaud them, some rebel, but usually there's a limit to how many of the state's enemies can be killed—or 'disappeared'—before the entire population feels threatened, and the system breaks down. Pol Pot conceived his own unique ideology. His idea was to remove Cambodia from time and history.

In other words, erase the past few centuries and immerse his country in a . . . what's the word . . . 'rural' system. To change all the members of the populace, be they executives, cooks or office workers, into farmers. Or dead people. I don't think what the Khmer Rouge did was morally worse than death squads in Guatemala, the genocides in Rwanda, or the ethnic cleansing in Yugoslavia. Those kinds of horrors aren't unique to Cambodia. But for some reason here, a large number of young people—many of them were no more than children—became convinced that they were Pol Pot's only true believers. Everyone else, from their point of view, was the enemy. And they put those enemies to death in inconceivable numbers. A million, maybe even two . . ."

"I don't want to hear those stories anymore," Camila says in frustration. "I don't want to think about those Khmers. I want the ones from hundreds of years ago, the ones who built those temples and carved on them. Or the ones we saw in the lake, with canoes full of flowers and produce. I don't want to hear that those Khmers, the ones we saw, are capable of killing thousands of people. I won't believe it."

"I don't think they would be," David says. "I think they are—were—victims of the Khmer Rouge, survivors of that hideous time. That's why the red bandanas bother me. I wonder who it is that might be wearing them."

"You talk about Guatemala, Rwanda, all those other places. People die all over as you said. . . . What's your special interest in Cambodia?" Márgara asks.

"I'm not obsessed with tales of slaughter, I promise you that," David says. "I didn't seek Cambodia out. In a way it found me. My father died here."

David says nothing more. He lights a pipe, then sips from his glass. Suddenly neither Camila nor Márgara have any more questions.

"I think we need to cheer up," Camila says. "Will you play for us please, David?"

David goes to the piano. He seems so absent that after a long while, Márgara and Camila leave without saying good-night.

Good-bye to Angkor

David appears as usual at breakfast and informs Márgara and Camila that he has important matters to attend to. He'll be back for lunch. So they decide to take the morning off. They arrange themselves by the pool along with their books, magazines, sunglasses, and lotion. Márgara glances up from a page to find her sister staring off, her gaze fixed on the water.

"What do you hear from Bobby?" Márgara says.

"He hasn't called for two days," Camila says. "He left Frankfurt for who-knows-where and said he'd let me know when he got back." Thinking on it, Márgara realizes she hasn't heard her brother-in-law's faithful ring in a while, the little bell at the end of the thread that still connects them.

"We need to know where to meet him," Márgara says.

"Are you tired of your temples already?"

"It's not that," Márgara says. "I don't think I could ever get tired of them. Still we have to make plans, figure out where we're going next."

Camila is different around David. She's different around any man. What Márgara would really like is some neutral time, and more than that a neutral place. A truly man-free no-man's land with nothing going on, where she can get a clear sense for what's been happening underneath Camila's indifferent exterior during all this time away from her husband.

"Do you miss him?" Márgara asks.

"Who?" says Camila.

"What do you mean who? Bobby."

"Oh, I'm used to it. He travels so much. And anyway, everything is so fascinating here."

"The place or the man?"

"Both of course," she says. "Who can deny what a fascinating man David is?"

"And attractive on top of it," Márgara says. "And then there's a curtain of mystery; it makes him seem even more so. I hope you haven't let yourself be seduced by it."

"You have to live what comes your way," Camila says. "That's what Bobby likes to say."

"I can't believe you," Márgara says. "That's outrageous."

"You're a fine one to talk," Camila says. "As if you haven't been flirting with him."

Márgara is about to retort, but for some reason she stops herself. Stop playing the disapproving older sister, Márgara. It's neither appropriate nor fair. Anyway she's right: you do flirt with David. And what about him? Márgara would like to believe that deep down he'd really like to be with her. The mere thought that she'd find that pleasing makes her so mad she throws down her book and jumps into the pool. She swims with long rhythmic strokes. Doing it that way, swimming for the sake of swimming, it feels like walking. She never tires. So much family folklore. Camila and her impossible boyfriends, Márgara and her nonexistent ones. They don't really hold up to reality. No one, after all, was more impossible than Arturo. So much so that Camila never even knew he existed. Shame on you, Margarita (she always scolds herself in the diminutive). Here you are trying to maintain your status as the sensible sister. What a hypocrite you are. How was it that you, the logical one, the reasonable one, fell in love with an impossible man, one more absurd than any of Camila's conquests. And what made him so absurd? The fact that he was married. The memory upsets her so much that she quickens her pace. In time she begins to tire and is forced to slow down again. Arturo the Unpredictable. With a wife, children, two jobs: his real one and the one at their illusory magazine. A businessman and an historian remade as self-styled political scientists. What hope could there have been for a project so pretentious when its owner and its editor, on top of being inexperienced, were caught up in the middle of a whirlwind romance? He seduced her, drew away and came back again like a pendulum, with an ambivalence that was so frustratingly masculine. Oh how easily we fall back on clichés when we need them. And you, oh Rock of Gibraltar amid all the currents, holding so tightly to your false serenity. It was an affair happening in another time, or so you told him, with neither a future nor consequences. What a delicious lie that was, that phony detachment. You always carried him close to you, so close he pressed against your skin. Every dress you bought you got so he could see you in it. You unfailingly wore the same perfume so its scent would remind him of you. You reflexively relive scenes of love and anger. I love you and I never want to see you again, words as passionate as they were repetitive. A failed crystallization. Long after the thaw, when you got so you recognized the mood swings and the absences that would follow, you knew he would come and find you. It's all what they call—or at least you call—compassionate maturity. How pathetically trite. Good God, it's nothing but simple stupidity. An adolescent falling-in-love. And at your age. Then maybe it was the sex? The affection, the laughter. Oh hurry up and justify yourself, Margarita. Suddenly, as she was about to make a turn, she feels something holding her by the swimsuit straps.

"You are the reincarnation of the *nagas*," a muffled voice says. Clutching the side, she sees David squatting by the pool, offering her his hand.

"Based on what I've seen, you could have made it at least half-way across the English Channel by now." He wraps her in one towel and rubs her hair with a smaller one. Squinting into the sun, she sees Camila sleeping on a lounge chair, a magazine on the ground.

"I must have been in the water for quite a while," Márgara says. "I lost track of time."

"Don't ever do that in the ocean," David says. "It's almost lunch time. Come on, I ordered you a vodka tonic."

"What's your family like, David?" Camila asks. "That marvelous brother you never talk about." She grasps a glass of cognac with both hands and reclines on the lounge chair she's been in all day.

"He's a terrific guy," David says. "Though I only found that out later on, as I think I told you. My parents divorced early and, you know, you have to give your children the best education you can. Then again maybe we were just in our mother's way. She was a pretty single woman. Anyway, he and I were hustled from one boarding school to the next for most of our lives."

"Did either of your parents remarry?"

"My mother did," David says. "To a man who really was a good friend to us. With him in the picture we were home a lot more. What about your husband, Camila? What does he do?" David asks, switching subjects.

"He's a business man who spoils me," Camila says.

"Spoiling you is his business?" David asks.

"Practically," Camila laughs, lying back completely. "You might say he's a professional spoiler, right Márgara?"

"You might say that," Márgara says, nodding repeatedly. Her eyes are growing sleepy. We've had too much to drink, she thinks. She stretches her legs to wake them up.

"He's an extreeeeemly successful business man," Camila says. "He travels a lot. So much that I always have a bag packed, so I can leave at a moment's notice when he decides to take me with him. And then . . . he spoils me. That's why we're here. We left him in Frankfurt. But who knows where he is now, off on some sort of important business." Camila says slowly, pronouncing each syllable with care. The only one of them who seems completely sober is David, though his eyes are sparkling a bit more than usual.

"How lucky am I?" Camila says. "It's because of him we can all spend our days here together.

"And you, Márgara-Margarita?" David asks. "What do you do when you're not traveling?"

"Oh, I'm a hard-working girl," Márgara says. "I don't travel much. Or at any rate I used to be."

"You used to be what, hard working?" David asks.

"Right, a hard-working historian," Márgara says. "But I left my job to start a magazine that died; it died. . . ."

"A magazine about what?" David asks.

"Politics," Márgara says. "Which is something you should never, never do . . . very complicated. We gave the thing a decent burial right before I left. The poor thing was so ill . . . terminally ill, really."

"Now I see why you get so excited about history," David says. "You take a professional interest in it also."

Camila sits up and holds out her glass for David to refill.

"Oh now, don't go getting all serious on me," Camila says. "Enough with the history. What happened to the story we were telling?"

"That's right, we've abandoned our characters," David says. "Will you pick up where we left off, Márgara?"

"No way," Márgara says. "I'm in no condition to tell stories. But you look coherent David."

"Less so than you might think," David says.

"As I recall," Márgara says, "you left Francisco in the middle of the West with a bunch of rough-and-tumble gun-slinging cowboys. Is the poor guy going to die out there?"

"Of course he can't die," David says. "He has to get back and get married to your great-grandma. Or your great-great-grandma, or something like that, right?"

"True enough," Márgara says. "He can't die. . . ."

"What do you think our great-grandmas did all shut up in their houses while their husbands-to-be just came and went?" Camila asks rhetorically. "No boyfriends, nothing but dogs, cats, canaries . . . embroidery, knitting. Just a bunch of grumpy old maids. Yuck." She wrinkles her nose in disgust.

"They got all hot and bothered reading Boccaccio," Márgara says.

"Oh c'mon, Márgara," Camila says. "Admit it. They'd just fall in love with another woman!" David laughs. Márgara merely raises her eyebrows.

"I wouldn't have the slightest idea," Márgara says. "But I do know *that* would never have been allowed."

"We're not talking about propriety, we're talking necessity," Camila insists. "I'll bet they weren't as innocent as we think. They'd never have admitted it, of course. Just became infatuated with each other."

"A love that dare not speak its name?" David asks. "But I can imagine people of that time. Wound up Victorians in one sense, a bunch of hippy free lovers in another."

"I hate that kind of talk," says Márgara. "It demeans the whole concept of freedom."

"All right, point taken," David says. "They were hypocrites then. Though I prefer to imagine an innocent, romantic Camila," says David.

"Two synonyms for ignorant?" Camila asks, indignant.

"Maybe by our standards, Camila," David says. "Those were different times."

"Well there they are, at any rate," says Márgara. "Stuck. An innocent, romantic Camila, and a Francisco that's what, free? What are you going to do with him David? He has to find some passion out there in his wanderings."

"I'll have to think about it," David says. "A freckled frontierswoman with the hands of a longshoreman. Or a chorus girl in a red dress with a plunging neck line."

"Ooh, I know," says Camila. "Maybe a gambler like him."

"I promise I'll work on it," David says. "I'm no good today. By tomorrow I'll have come up with something."

Márgara feels dizzy, about to drift off to sleep. She takes her leave with a mumbled 'good night' looking dubiously over at the staircase leading up to their room.

The next thing she knows, a hand is shaking her awake.

"Márgara! Márgara! Get up! David left," the same hand draws back the blinds. The brightness hurts. "Look, he left us this." She dangles the note in front of her face. Márgara rubs her eyes. She can feel lasts night's cigarettes grating on her throat. She has a monumental headache.

"David left? When?" she asks.

"I don't know, probably early this morning," Camila says. She holds out the note out to her. "He left the jeep and a driver to take us wherever we want to go."

Márgara spends the day at Angkor Thom. Mostly at Ta Prohm, in the smaller temples she hadn't visited before. It feels like a good-bye, though curiously lacking in nostalgia for the thing she is about to leave. That will come later, she knows, but for now the feeling is of a time that's reached its proper end. The Cambodian driver smiles and does her bidding silently. He lets her lose herself in the moment without interruption. Maybe this is how she should have first seen this place, led by a mute and obliging guide. No distractions. She'd asked the hotel kitchen to prepare a lunch. She shared with the driver, seated beneath a tree. He didn't understand when she asked him his name and she felt too embarrassed to ask a second time. He attempted some historical commentary but his English was barely comprehensible. She responded with brief praise of the site, but in the end their exchanges were mostly limited to smiles. Only after many hours did he finally point to his watch and say 'sunset'. Without another word he took her to Angkor Wat and pointed upward. She followed him up the stairs to the highest terrace and offered him a cigarette. They waited in silence until the last rays of sunlight disappeared. Thank you, she said. He responded by pressing his hands together, a gently bowing of his head. A *namaste.*

On the way back to the hotel, the swaying of the jeep puts Márgara briefly to sleep. She wakes up when they reach the entrance, and it takes her a moment to remember where she is. This happens when she travels. She wakes up in a hotel bed surrounded by unfamiliar furniture and it takes her a few minutes to figure out her whereabouts. Saying goodbye to her guide leaves her with a sense of loss. She wants to tell him that she's leaving, that she won't be seeing him again, but their common vocabulary is far too limited. The man nevertheless seems to intuit it. "Bon voyage," he says. Too late she realizes that she might have been able to speak to him in French, though she never really sought any deeper communication. She tells the desk attendant that they won't be needing Mr. Masters-Iturbe's jeep any longer, is told that the vehicle will be waiting for the gentleman when he returns. She calls their room from the bar. It rings forever. Finally a damp-sounding Camila answers and tells her she'll come down as soon as she's dressed. She had refused to accompany her that morning. "I have to find Bobby, Márgara. We're hours ahead. I don't want to rush." Hours ahead of what, she asks. "Of the office in Mexico City, he wouldn't have called home if he knew I wouldn't be there. His secretary should know how to find him. Anyway I want to take my time packing." Oh well, maybe they both needed a little time alone. She's enjoyed hers immensely.

"Did you find Bobby?" Márgara asks.

"No," Camila says.

"What do you mean, doesn't his office know anything?"

"He left a message that if I called, we should say where we're going to be and he'll get in touch."

"Why didn't he call here?"

"Christ, Márgara, you've simply never understood Bobby," Camila says impatiently. "He's a very busy man."

"But if he's got time to call his office. . . ." She's sorry the moment the words come out of her mouth. She doesn't finish the sentence. Don't go getting mixed up in what's none of your business, Márgara. Or at any rate don't make it more obvious.

"Are we going back to Mexico?" Márgara asks.

"No, we have to wait for him here." Camila says.

"Here? In Siem Reap?"

“No not here, I mean around here. I figured it out. I’ve got two tickets to Bangkok for tomorrow. We’ll go to Bali.”

“Camila, this is absurd. Are we just going to wander around Asia waiting for your husband to turn up?” There’s an expression on her sister’s face that Márgara doesn’t recognize. Her voice loses its edge.

“But you know, what do I know? I’m the guest, your lady in waiting. So let’s go to Bali. Though I could think of a few better places . . .”

“You’re sweet, Márgara. I’d forgotten what a good time I have with you. Look, see? I have reservations at the Four Seasons.” She pushes a pamphlet across the table covered with photos of beaches and blue seas. “We should leave some instructions here for Bobby and David.”

“Forget about David,” Márgara says. “He could be in Mexico or Timbuktu for all we know.”

“But his note his says he’ll catch up with us. . . .”

“David says a lot of things.”

“I’m sure that he’ll come and find us. He’s interested in you, Márgara.”

“Or maybe you’re interested in him?”

“No, he likes you. I know all about it, but don’t ask me to explain it to you now.”

Bali

Balí

When we last left our hero he was engaged in conversation with one Don Pedro de Guzmán, a Spanish gentleman, or so he called himself. Given the precarious nature of the spot he'd landed in, Francisco was only too happy to take his leave and travel with Don Pedro to Mohawk. He wasn't sure if Mohawk was the name of a city or a territory, but Guzmán seemed the most civilized of all available options. And anyway, he had to leave there one way or another; this way he'd be accompanied. The first thing Guzmán did was take him to get a horse. It was a restless appaloosa named Gunshot, a name that horrified him, but Guzmán wouldn't let him change it (changing horses' names brings you bad luck). He also saw to it that Francisco bought a saddle and saddlebags. Francisco regretted not having brought one of his father's shotguns, or better still a revolver. "We'll get one in Mohawk," Guzmán told him. They spent two days crossing the plains. He learned to start fires at sundown, how to balance a can of coffee on the rocks, even how to cook meat over the coals, whatever meat that might be. Guzmán was a crack shot, but as for the critters he hit, Francisco preferred not to know. Thinking about those brave days, of galloping over open ground, makes me deeply envious. I've always dreamt of speeding across those landscapes on horseback, riding hard under the Western sun. As for Francisco, each night he found himself exhausted. Still, it wasn't easy to sleep. The archetypal tenderfoot, he could feel every last one of the seven hundred stones under his back. The sky twinkled with stars he'd never seen. "They must be the same ones I see in my country," he said to his compadre. "Don't you believe it, boy," said Guzmán. "The desert makes things up as it goes along." On the third day the Earth beneath him seemed to wrinkle. Hills surged up to their right, then reddish mountain ranges off in the distance. I think of him sitting upright on his horse, his gaze lost over the horizon. He'd never experienced such beautiful solitude. That same day they saw a long line of riders along a hilltop. "Injuns," murmured Guzmán, "Probably Apache. Don't you worry, boy. We're nothing to them."

The town of Mohawk consisted of one long dusty street. It was lined with wooden houses that were connected by one continuous porch, two or three steps above the ground. Here and there signs were hung: Bank, Post Office, Dentist, *Palace Hotel and Saloon.* They made straight for the bar. Hitching their horses to the rail, Guzmán promptly disappeared behind a pair of strange shuttered half-doors. Francisco slowly realized he was right back where he'd started: a saloon. He went in. The bar ran the length of the place. Behind it was a barkeep with a long moustache. There were tables with people drinking and playing cards, and in a corner, a man at a piano. Beside him a woman was singing: the most beautiful woman Francisco had ever seen. She wore a black dress with a plunging neckline, her hair gathered at the neck. He was stunned. "Who is that?" he whispered to Guzmán. "No one, boy, just some singer." They approached the bar. While Guzmán started up a conversation with the barkeep, Francisco took stock of the mystery woman. Huge brown eyes, locks of hair falling down her bare shoulders. Bright red lips and a tiny waist. "What is her name?" he asked the bartender. "You must be new around here, son," the man said to him. "Her name's Emma."

"That's not fair, David," says Márgara. "There's my poor great-grandma, doing nothing but dreaming about him, and that son of a bitch is off getting all lathered up over somebody else?"

"You have to meet this girl," David says. "What a woman. And in what way is he being a son of a bitch? He's got no idea that some crazy dame back home is pining for him. He doesn't even remember her."

"What nerve! Yours I mean, not his."

"Oh, let him enjoy his freedom."

"So he gets all the freedom while she's got nothing but her imagination. But then where can you have better adventures? In the old West or in your own mind?"

"That's some question. I don't know. At least in fantasyland you don't have to worry about being shot full of holes. But quit interrupting me. My muse is slipping away. So okay, Emma was singing and Francisco couldn't take his eyes off her. Guzmán's thinking: a fine partner I've gone and found for myself! The first floozy he runs into, and she stops him dead in his tracks. This dandy (such a nice word, don't you think?) is useless. But he was mistaken. He wasn't useless and she wasn't a floozy, as we'll soon see. When the music ended Francisco grabbed a bottle and two glasses from the bar, went over to the woman and introduced himself: Francisco Videgaray, at your service, he said, and bowed slightly. She looked him over: his build, his clothes, his manner. Not the kind of thing you see every day in these parts. . . ."

I never thought I had any story-telling ability. But for some reason this character brought it out. Or maybe it was the place. Such are the fantasies of my generation. We all wanted to be cowboys, not exploring the North Pole or sailing up the Yang-Tse. The Wild West, the source of the Nile—one you find in the movies, the other you find in books. Here we are in one of the most mythic regions in the world and we're spending our time dreaming up stories that are set somewhere else. Maybe it's a way to find ourselves. If we do it in fantasy first then maybe we can do it in reality later. Or maybe we just need something to give us some sense of purpose through all this absurd waiting. And it really is absurd you know, for her more than it is for me. I still can't fathom such blind loyalty. Such passive acceptance of someone else's designs. There must be some underlying reason I haven't glimpsed yet, some need to create a void, a transition between one moment and another. Does it matter if I'm here? If I weren't, would she just go off to Paris? Or back to Mexico? Maybe leave Camila to chase that elusive husband of hers around the globe? Mysteries, mysteries. I wonder if this crazy story about their ancestors might bridge that gap. Could chasing mirages across the Western plains serve any purpose? Maybe to erase other mirages, or to create a few new ones. . . .

"Emma gestured to an empty table where they went to sit down, she with a wry smile and he with a look of utter amazement. They talked about the things people always talk about when they first make contact with one another. His gaze drifted back and forth between her brown eyes and her neckline, which interfered with his train of thought quite a bit. Suddenly two characters appeared out of nowhere and greeted her like old friends. Are you playing, Emma? they asked. Francisco looked confused while she stared pointedly at them, her eyebrows raised in silent questioning. Without waiting for an answer, both men sat down at the table. One of them produced a deck of cards older than Methusaleh. Marked for sure, Francisco said to himself. But, since I'm here. . . . Emma muttered two names as introduction, Tom-something and another one he couldn't hear. Still, no one held out a hand, so he simply imitated their grunt of a greeting. The game began in genteel fashion, cards changed hands politely. But, little by little, the balance tipped in Emma's favor. Each time she lay down a winning hand, she shot Francisco a glance, conspiratorial yet vaguely defiant. As we said, Francisco was amazed, not stupefied. She wants me to follow her. Alright then, I'm game, let's play for real. He pulled a fresh deck out of his bag. Now it's my turn to cheat. She winked, discreetly. Remember now that Francisco had always been a loner. But suddenly he found himself complementing her game; counting her cards, reacting to what she'd throw, being careful to let their adversaries win back enough so they wouldn't get suspicious. This was really a thrill. A partner and a rival all in one. Being more knowledgeable about the place, she slowly withdrew, letting Francisco take the lead. He got the message that they needn't embarrass these two. They let the pair recover the smallest part of their losses, enough to end the game in peace.

"You really know how to play," she told him later when they were alone. I imagine he wanted to tell her that cards weren't all he was good at. Anyway, that's what I would have said."

"Men."

"Well, it's important to let people know the things you're good at."

"Better to let other people point them out to you."

"How's that going to happen if you never have the opportunity to show them off? Take me for instance, so far the only thing you know about me is that I happen to be a good storyteller."

"That's not true, you're also an excellent guide. You play the piano pretty well. . . ."

"Oh, go on. But those aren't what I'm best known for."

"What then?"

"That's for you to find out. For now I'll continue with the story. Until now I had no idea of its potential."

"What, literary potential?"

"Don't distract me. This is a very important moment. Francisco took Emma by the hand and led her back to the piano. She sat down beside him, fiddled with the keys a bit, then sang a bunch of melancholy tunes he'd never heard before. At first the crowd would applaud when Emma finished a song, though the applause eventually died away when the audience realized she wasn't paying attention to them. When Emma left her hand hanging in the air at the end of an arpeggio, Francisco took it and kissed it. He took her by the waist, drew her close and kissed her. It obviously didn't bother Francisco much, kissing a girl in front of the entire Wild West, something Emma must have clearly understood, for without saying a word she took him by the hand and led him up the stairs to her room. Francisco was utterly oblivious to everything around him. Everything, that is, except the woman undressing in front of him.

"And?"

"Use your imagination."

"Oh you're not going to stop now. . . ."

"Of course I am. I'm no good at sex scenes."

"Oh, I hate you. I can't decide if you're a trouble maker or a hypocrite."

"Neither. Now let's go find a piano."

"There isn't one."

"It's a metaphor."

Márgara waits for David to wake up. Her face, moist with perspiration, is resting on his shoulder. Morning light is filtering in through the horizontal lines of the shutters, bringing heat with it. She draws away enough so she can see their clothes lying on the chair near the foot of the bed. She tries to sit up but his arm, slack and heavy on her body, weighs her down. She settles back down and mentally flips through the images of the previous night. He took her hand and kissed it. Then without a word he guided her along the garden path to his room. He drew her near and kissed her. He said he was no good at telling scenes like this, though he never stopped whispering while he untied her belt, slipped the dress up over her shoulders and let it fall. I just had to come find you, was the only thing she remembered hearing. In a flash, the memory of other hands comes back to her, his way of standing back a little so he could see all of her. David travels her body slowly, as if in an attempt to leave his image imprinted on her skin. She responds slowly. She needs to take the excitement in first, to assimilate it before she's able to act. He fumbles with his own clothing, not wanting to break contact, to stop touching her. Their naked bodies grow impatient. He finds the bed blindly, then lays down beside her and wraps her in his arms. He raises her gently until she's on top of him, looking into his eyes. Why have we waited so long? he whispers. His smile in some way frees her. Her hands lose their stiffness and caress him, guiding his lips. There isn't one echo now, only David and his anxious sex.

Márgara waits for David to wake up. She waits, I wait. I've been waiting for David to seduce me, for Camila to come back, or not come back, so I can stop waiting for her. My great-grandma Camila waited. Meanwhile I have

David painting a portrait of a Francisco who might not want to come back. I hate that infinitive: to wait. It's all inertia and indecision. Camila doesn't wait. She never did. She just carries on stumbling, quarreling. Though now she's the one who's waiting. Expectant, docile, ready to be led, called to the mystery. It's a mystery to me, anyway. I waited, I waited way too long. I couldn't pursue David until he'd already decided on me. I crouch down and hide until events arrive, until other people bring my life to me. Did I know this was going to happen? Glances, touches, coincidences. But it's Camila, with her magnet-colored eyes, who's always the obvious choice, while I keep my distance. Afraid of awakening ghosts, of thawing out. Who is he? Who are we, stranded here for no reason? Though he seems to have one. Camila does too, though isn't she being dragged along by someone else? And I'm being dragged along by . . . who? Might as well be me. No more rationalizations, no more questions.

Márgara waits for David to wake up. His sleep is so deep she manages to slip from under his arm and out of bed. She looks for her dress, and finding it wrinkled on the floor, decides to look through his drawers for a shirt. Standing upright puts things back in their proper place. This room is the same as hers, but a little neater. The remains of last night, sandals beneath the armchair, a pair of pants flung over the back, are all that disturb the harmony. She could snoop around a little for . . . what? A briefcase? The kind you handcuff to your wrist? A high-powered rifle with a telescopic sight? A suitcase full of money? Little bags of white powder? A drawer full of passports? All the same pictures but with different names? Oh you're such an idiot, Margarita. Or is it that you'd rather have some kind of grand adventure—perhaps in an Asian prison, the kind Americans like putting in movies, complete with rats, cockroaches, a thug, and water seeping down the walls? Better to simply ask questions like a civilized person. But he doesn't talk and you don't probe. The orange light gets steadily brighter. She feels like opening the blinds and going out to the balcony, to gaze across the jungle below. She finds the electric coffee pot on the dresser but hesitates. *Colombian coffee* a package label reads, and then there's some tea from who-knows where. Why is it always Colombian coffee in these places? Doesn't Bali make anything? Not Bali, you idiot, Indonesia. Oh right, rice. You've been driving past rice fields for days. She opts for imported coffee on the balcony, sliding the door open just enough to get out. The sun is already high, and the morning light reflected off the leaf sea nearly blinds her. What a delicious climate. She craves a cigarette, but that would mean rifling through pockets, drawers. . . . You're not in your own room, and if Camila were to call . . . there's that echo of anxiety again. That night when he finally called, it was during dinner. The bellman came to get her, though Camila decided to take the call in her room. She returned much later and announced simply, "I'm going to meet Bobby." David offered up a lame excuse and disappeared. Where? I have no idea, Márgara. And so, without further ado, she packed a few of her clothes (carefully, as she always does, so nothing would wrinkle and everything would be easy to find). In her turn, Márgara announced she was going back to Mexico. Suddenly, inexplicably, she found Camila weeping in her arms. What could be so wrong as to make Camila, the strong one, the optimist, cry? Wait for me, Márgara. What do you mean, wait for me? Where? For how long? For what? It's not forever, Márgara. Bobby has no way of knowing how long. . . . With an impatient wave of her hand she pulls away and flees to the bathroom. Márgara watches her wash her face and one by one open the series of bottles that constitute her nightly ritual: cream for her eyes, lotion for her neck, all applied in steady, rhythmic motions.

"Tell me what's going on, Camila," she says in an even voice, trying to imitate Camila's usual calm.

"I can't. I don't know. I'm only asking you for a few days, Márgara."

"A few days of what?"

"Of waiting. If I don't come back or call in a week, go back to Mexico."

"You're crazy. How do you expect me to leave without knowing where you are or what's happened to you? Tell me truthfully. Bobby's in trouble?"

"I think so."

"Drugs?"

"Now you're the one who's crazy. How could you even think something like that?" Camila is shouting now.

"I'm sorry, but he's the one with the mysterious behavior. The strange hours, the sudden trips. We're in a part of the world where those kinds of things happen, you know? The Golden Triangle: Myanmar, Laos, it's not exactly a stretch. This isn't Wall Street. We're not on the Silk Road and Bobby's no Marco Polo. Do you have any idea what he does for a living? And do you have any idea what could happen to you?"

Camila wipes the tears and moisturizing cream from her face and sits down on the edge of the tub.

"It's nothing like that. You don't have to worry about me. The situation isn't that bad, Márgara. More like financial problems."

"His?"

"Not exactly. . . . Bobby's an investor. He manages money

for people, off-shore accounts, fiscal paradises, you know. . . ."

"No, I don't know. But I can imagine. Are you involved?"

"Oh come on. Look ..." she goes over to the night table and produces her passport. She opens it and shows it to her sister. "You didn't notice did you? I use my maiden name, even when I travel. See? Bobby protects me."

"Oh, Camila, I hope so . . . but what are you doing? What are we doing here? And where is he?"

"I can't tell you. But believe me, things are bad. He wants to see me. In a few days everything will be all fixed up, I'm sure of it. We'll come back, pick you up, and go back to Mexico."

"And if it doesn't get all fixed up?"

"I'll call you and you can go."

"Perfect. I leave and you stay here, a fugitive from justice."

"I promise I'll call and tell you what's happening. He already explained everything to me yesterday. If things don't settle down we'll find a safe place to stay until we can go home."

"A safe place . . . like a jail?"

"Don't say a thing like that."

"Why not? I'm furious! To think that a con artist like Bobby would drag you into his shady dealings . . . and you follow him!"

"He's my husband and I love him."

"Oh don't be so Victorian. Stay with me and let him come find you when he can. If he's still interested."

But it was useless. Camila put on the impassive mask she wears so well, and slept soundly while her sister tossed and turned. In the morning she got up, got dressed and put on make-up as if she were leaving for a press interview. She declined all offers to escort her to the airport. Márgara had to restrain David on that front, as he was determined to take her in his car. Let her go, she doesn't want company. He looked at her, confused. Now alone they together forced themselves to ignore the obvious questions that buzzed around them like horseflies. He took note of her silence, her fleeting glances, and suggested they go to Ubud instead of spending the day on the beach as they'd planned. They say it's a very pleasant place, the mountains. Besides I saw the brochure for a hotel that you're going to like.

What a strange trajectory. A few days after they arrived in Bali, she and Camila rented a car and picked up the British habit of driving on the left. It's impossible to travel on highways that scarcely deserve the name. Rather it's like they're on one never-ending street that connects one town to another. After too many hours and too few kilometers, multiple driver changes (in hopes that one of them might be more competent than the other), and terrified by the prospect of running down a pedestrian, a cyclist or a pole, they returned, heads hung in shame, to hand over the keys in the hotel office. The desk clerk chuckled good-naturedly. Tourists always say they want to drive but, like I said, it's better to hire a driver. Oh, we can handle it, they'd smugly announced that morning. The next time you ladies want to go out, let me know the night before and I'll get you a driver. They agreed. Sometimes you just have to face up to your limitations. David, by comparison, didn't agonize over the experience. He adeptly dodged obstacles: cars, humans, dogs. He even kept up a coherent conversation. The term is relative of course, since they were both trying so hard not to mention the unmentionable. They dodged those topics just as neatly, going round and round with inoffensive prattle. How about those rice stalks? Pretty high aren't they? And good for you, too.

I'm told they make some dynamite furniture here these days. I'll bet the hotels of Asia, Africa, and Oceania are stuffed with it. But they'll be damned if they can find a simple wood carving either of them are happy with. Finally, David puts an end to the inanity: don't worry about it Márgara, we'll talk about it. At the time she doesn't bother to inquire as to what "it" is. But somehow his comment sets them free.

And suddenly here they are in Ubud. They wander down the steep, narrow streets. He presents her with some brightly-colored wooden fish, then insists on buying her an amber and bone necklace. Next he makes her try on dresses until she finds a cotton tunic—the one that at this very moment is draped over the chair in David's room. That night in the hotel bar David starts telling the story again, as if he'd only left off yesterday. Evidently there was a motive behind it. But then looking back it was probably inevitable, even without the story. Everything has converged, Camila's leaving, this neutral ground. No, that's not right, this . . . but then this city of Ubud and this hotel with its thatched huts and jungle offers no clear reference points. They're isolated. If Camila were here . . . but, it doesn't matter. She's not. The absurdity of all that waiting in Bali after they'd left Angkor! Waiting for the phone to ring, for somebody to show up.

The first phantom to materialize was David, against all logic. He simply appeared on the beach one morning and sat down on the sand beside them. No one asked any questions, which to Márgara completed the surrealistic picture. Come on Márgara, pull it together. It's that or leave yourself at the mercy of two crazy people. The first thing to do is to start asking questions, like any normal person would under the circumstances. But she didn't. They reverted to their Siem Reap routine, though it was shortly interrupted by Bobby's phone call. That did happen, didn't it? At the moment nothing seems real.

Márgara waits for David to wake up. And there he is, standing beside the sliding door, observing her. She's so lost in thought she doesn't even notice him.

You are one lucky son of a bitch. Who would have thought she'd let herself be left alone? That you'd have the chance to come here and be with her without her sister? Otherwise you'd have had to explain, postpone. Explaining yourself will be easy now, now that everything's fallen together. And the thing you need to explain (assuming it's really necessary to explain it) won't carry as much weight, even for you. It's just some nostalgic piece of history. What matters is her, right now. And you with her, if she's willing. If all the confusion doesn't scare her. But then she doesn't seem the skittish type. Prudent, rational Márgara.

The sound of his voice makes her jump. In the scant space of the balcony, David can just fit behind her chair, bend down, put his arms around her and kiss her on top of her head, her long hair tousled by the night. She turns her head to reach his lips, so she doesn't have to say anything. He grasps her by the elbows and helps her get up. Not much room out here, come on. He leads her by the hand back into the bedroom. Seeing the unmade bed he hesitates. Would my lady care to breakfast, he asks with a formal expression, at least until their eyes meet and he can't contain his laughter. She can't either, and they fall into each other's arms amid all the disorder. I'm going to take a bath, she announces. Can I move my things to your room then, he asks? That way we'll avoid wandering the hallways in our shirttails. . . .

At breakfast it suddenly hits Márgara: "We can't stay here. Camila doesn't know where I am."

"I don't mean to pry, but when did she tell you she'd call? And to say what?"

"I don't know, in a few days. It's all very ill-defined. What about you? Do you want to tell me what you're doing here?"

"I came to find you. Isn't it obvious?"

"I mean in Cambodia, in Asia."

He pauses. "I propose a deal. Let's give ourselves two days of vacation."

"Two? Didn't we just have twenty?"

"Not really. Two days here with nothing to do but enjoy ourselves, then back to Bali where we'll make complete confessions. Everything."

"Why the waiting?"

"Because I'm hoping that in two days you'll fall so deeply in love with me that nothing else will matter to you."

"That's the scariest thing I've heard so far. And the most egotistical. You think by then I'll just be some piece of furniture, ready to support any shady thing you may be up to?"

"There are no shady things, Margarita. Trust me."

Trust. . . . Did you trust Arturo? He didn't deserve it, but then you didn't really give him any. He was ambivalent and you were certain. You can trust this David person. Trust what? His honesty? The fact that he's not another Bobby, that he cares about you? If not, then why would he have bothered to come here? Abandoning whatever it is he was looking for or waiting for back there. There's probably more than a little bit of himself in his Francisco. If that's the case we are sending cryptic messages, because I am not either of the two Camilas. Could it be that someone is waiting for him back home and I'm the woman from the Wild West? Oh, don't complicate things—two days and a confession. But I don't know what you're going to confess. The only secret you have belongs to someone else. But he . . . oh, two days of your life, Márgara. There's no one else you'd rather spend them with. Deep down you knew that this was going to happen. You wanted it but were afraid it wouldn't be with you.

That day he makes love to her for a long time. The initial urgency having run its course, he takes time to get to know the territory he'd overrun so hastily the night before. She allows herself be led to a place beyond conscious thought, aware only of her body, which he brings to the limits of exhilaration as though he knew her. As though he knew. They have left the window open. Sleepily they watch the sun move up the sky until it's lost above the frame. We should go out, Márgara murmurs. What do you want to see in Ubud? I don't know, but my conscience objects to so much inactivity. Well, I don't know about you, but I for one have been very active. And besides, we've called a truce, right? From everything: from being travelers, from having to know every corner of a place. There's another type of corner I'm interested in right now. I'm going to call and order up something for lunch. Or dinner . . . whatever. Márgara wraps herself in one of the two cotton bathrobes left there by a prescient maid. How peculiar it must appear when tourists ask for two rooms but end up in only one. And they don't go out all day. Do you care? No. A table shortly appears. On it sits an arrangement of flowers from the gardens: wild, magnificent, intensely colored blooms, a bowl of fruit, a tray with a selection of fish and shellfish, and two bottles of wine in a frosted bucket. Now that I see all this I realize we haven't eaten all day. David, tell me a story.

"If I start telling stories and drinking wine I'll be asleep before you know it."

"Tell me more about Francisco. I'm interested in what happens to him."

"Francisco? Didn't I just get finished with the scene you were so interested in? Alive and in color no less. Not everything in the story lends itself to such vivid portrayals, I'll have you know. Parts of it get awfully murky. My source of information left quite a few gaps. So let me think now. Emma and Francisco wake up hungry, she asks that some food be brought up while he goes looking for the suitcase he left behind in the bar. Then he remembers: Guzmán. He asks a man he finds lazily sweeping the floor if anyone left a message for Francisco Videgaray. The most eloquent thing the man could muster was to spit, then kept on sweeping. Well, I guess that's that, he said to himself, and returned to Emma's room. He found her half-naked, with a corset full of ribbons, a white petticoat and boots, her long hair falling down to her waist, even prettier than when he had left her. That scene, of Emma sitting there on the bed in little else but her boots, would determine Francisco's future. From that moment on, he wouldn't be separated from her.

"Just like that? So fast?"

"Since when did love have a time limit? Francisco is a smitten man."

"So then what?"

"The story of Francisco and Emma is long and filled with intrigue. Unfortunately, it was never told to me in its entirety. But I can tell you the most important part. In fact, it's an important part of a legend that was only written down much later, when people began writing histories of the West. They were the most famous pair of gamblers that region had ever known. Emma had a, well, I suppose you might call him a bodyguard. An enormous black man named Sam who accompanied her everywhere she went. They say he'd looked after her since she was a little girl, ever since her parents died. The three of them stayed in Mohawk a few days, but it wasn't long before the local scene got a little too hot for them and they decided to move on. They packed up their horses at dawn. Just as he was about to mount, Francisco happened to look over and see Guzmán sitting on the hotel steps. Ever polite, he approached him to say good-bye. So you're leaving with the singer, he said. You're crazier than I thought, Videgaray, my boy. That's a sure-fire way to get yourself killed. But I'm not going to try to talk you out of it. Happy trails, sonny and good luck, and he embraced him. We'll see each other again. All roads go to the same place around here.

"In all his life, Francisco never knew anything like that trip he took with Emma. At sundown, when the sun hung like a red ball suspended in a golden desert haze, they would look for a place to camp. Sam looked after the horses while they tended to the fire, and fetched water for the coffee. Supper was an austere affair, usually what they could carry in their saddlebags. Occasionally an animal, if they could hunt one up before the darkness closed in around their glowing sphere of firelight. They drank rotgut straight from the bottle. Gradually the flames would die down leaving only embers to keep them company the rest of the night. Wrapped in his poncho a short distance away, Sam would play the harmonica while the coals glimmered. Such images would forever be etched into his memory, as would the feeling of lying naked beneath the traveling blanket, Emma's body arched beneath his, his hand over her mouth to drown out her scream. He never knew what Sam thought of him. Taciturn, silent Sam. The man who followed Emma with ferocious devotion. He barely spoke to Francisco, just monosyllables that bordered on hostility. He remarked on it to Emma, who tried to reassure him: as long as you make me happy, he'll be as devoted to you as he is to me. If you don't. . . . The elipses bothered him more than any specific threat would have. Who knows what personal definition of happiness that mastodon retained? And at what point he would see fit to punish signs of displeasure in his mistress? One tantrum and he sticks me in the middle of the night. But then Emma was the only reality he cared about, the copper dunes of her body by the light of the fire, the crazy thrill of rolling around with her in silence, with a witness so nearby. He saw her in the same way I see you, wanting to caress all of you, wanting to know you're mine. . . ." His voice fades off and his body speaks in its place. And Márgara becomes his.

Ubud turned out to be little more than a cloud-covered memory for both of them. Had some fact-hungry tourist asked them about it, they'd have said: there are lots of mountains and it's very green. Though in the mind's eye, all they would have seen was a bedroom, a bed, a window, and many hours of love making.

"This part of the story is mostly taken up with journeys from one town to another. Though 'town' isn't really the right word since most of the outposts they visited were only slightly more or less prosperous versions of Mohawk.

On arrival, Emma would don her best come-hither attire, and Francisco would change into something more or less typical of the locals. Sam simply slipped away (Francisco never ceased to be amazed at how such a mountainous person could vanish so easily). Their compatibility in bed (really just a euphemism since they rarely slept in one) was matched by their professional rapport. They were two sides of the same brain, able to communicate without speaking. Any passion they felt for one another during the game served to stoke the flame of what would come later. There were times when their burning glances made the table all but blaze. Other players were frequently compelled to abandon their seats. But a card table is no place for the timid, it being a territory of entrapment and seduction. Or maybe obsession is the better term. I should point out at this juncture that I'm not speaking from experience, since I'm a mediocre player at best. Though there was a time where I was tempted. . . .

"Then one day Emma presented him with a silver-handled revolver. It's from your country, she said. He carried it with him wherever he went. When they were on the trail, Emma wore a two-gun holster and carried a backup rifle wrapped in her bed roll. Sam likewise carried two pistols and a rifle, as well as a large knife (the one he feared might protrude from his back one day) concealed in a boot. Francisco frequently wondered exactly where and how such an arsenal might get used. In most towns they visited, signs on the main street announced a municipal prohibition against firearms. Francisco always found that amusing. Like almost all rules, it seemed directed at peaceful townsfolk who'd be inclined to follow it. Every delinquent and troublemaker that hit town simply ignored it, and the local sheriffs tended to avoid confronting them. Before heading down to the gaming parlor, Emma tucked a little single-shot derringer in her garter. The placement of that weapon produced distracting, turbulent images in Francisco. All he could think of was tearing it off her leg garter, stocking and all. At the same time he was conscious of the fact that the gun wasn't just some erotic decoration, that it had a use. But then if things got ugly, if one of the rival players that they routinely bilked put up a genuine fuss, what good would that little thing do them? What could he, as an unarmed accomplice do that wouldn't elicit more laughter than fear? But then playing the fool was the least of his worries. There was the real danger of dying a painful death staring at the underside of a gaming table. Emma intuited all of this, even though his pride wouldn't allow him to confess it.

"Many mornings were spent teaching him how to shoot. Francisco had decent aim, but never imagined he'd ever have to draw, aim, and fire a revolver in one seamless motion. How did you learn to do it? Sam taught me. And in fact Sam did observe the lessons, also from at a distance, randomly blowing his harmonica and shaking his head every time Francisco dropped his sidearm. Despite it all, in time Emma was able to turn him into plausible imitation of a gunfighter."

"How do you know so much about the Wild West? Are you some descendant of Billy the Kid?"

"Maybe I'm in fact the reincarnation of your ancestor."

"Puh-lease."

"Oh, it's a joke. But you'd be surprised at how many crystals-gazing freaks there are out there channeling Nero in their spare time."

"Isn't it true? Instead of evolving we're reverting back to witchcraft."

"My theory is that institutions of all kinds are losing prestige these days. A lot of people are frightened of being alone. The type of person who's used to following along needs somewhere to turn when it all comes tumbling down. Something to help them understand the world."

"There's no way to understand the world, but I think you have to trust in intelligence on some level."

"Well, aren't you the idealist? Crystals and séances are much more reassuring. At least if you're an ostrich."

"The problem I think isn't with understanding the world, but avoiding death. The great beyond, with all its prizes and punishments, reincarnation and crystals lets you avoid dealing with all that. They let you pretend it isn't there."

"Someone once said that man is the only animal who knows he's going to die. I guess you're right. The notion of another life (and if there was one before there would have to be one after) really is the ultimate carrot. You never reach it but it's always dangling in front of you, fodder for dreams."

"Well anyway, you never did tell me how you came to know so much about the West."

"Margarita, what you're getting is a rehash of all the cowboy movies I've ever seen in my life. The story of Francisco that I'm telling you may be the only Western I know that's true.

"One night, while the pair were resting in a hotel in some anonymous town, Sam knocked on the door of their room and asked Emma to come out. Francisco heard the two of them speaking in low tones. When she came back she had a serious expression on her face. Four-Aces Jack is here, she said, and he's waiting for us downstairs. Pharmacists generally don't have names like that, Francisco thought to himself. He's the best gambler in the West, Emma told him, mean as a snake and handy with a six-gun. We'll have to play this one straight, and if he beats us, so be it, Francisco said. Emma was furious. How could you even think such a thing? What about my reputation? If I had to choose between my reputation and my life. . . .

"Four-Aces Jack was as lean and gnarly as a desert willow, with an air of malicious authority. His moustache, barely a black line, traced thin lips. He pointed to two chairs opposite him and threw two new packs of cards down on the table. Emma gave him her most seductive smile and held out her hand (which the man barely touched). Francisco decided this was no time for niceties and took his seat with a customary grunt. Silently they dealt the cards. The only sound, the scratching of a match as Jack lit his cigar. This is like the Roman Coliseum, Francisco thought. We go around and around for a while and then the lion eats us. But I'm here to tell you they didn't get eaten. Throwing all caution to the wind, Francisco and Emma played like they never had before. Little by little, a circle of spectators began to surround the table. Before long they'd stripped their adversary of his every last cent. At that point Four-Aces Jack got up, gathered his cards and left without saying a word. Emma's eyes sparkled and Francisco congratulated himself for his triumph.

"Sam soon put a stop to all that. In uncharacteristic style he burst into their room and lambasted them for their stupidity. Roughly he began stuffing Emma's belongings into her saddlebags. We leave at daybreak, he said, before they gun you down right in front of my eyes, because I'm not about to stand up for a couple of idiots. Four-Aces Jack doesn't like being humiliated in public, especially by two cheaters. It was an episode that changed their journey. From then on Sam would have to nose around every saloon they happened upon to gather the latest rumors. It was always the same: They're on our trail, we have to go. Francisco suggested confronting the enemy, but for once

Emma showed some good sense. There's no way, Francisco, he's too good and he travels with a bunch of killers. Even if one of us could draw down on him, the rest of his gang would kill us. And here, unfortunately, the thread of my story runs out. To keep ahead of Four-Aces Jack they were forced to range further and further away. They traveled to California, and eventually went East where they made a name for themselves playing on the Mississippi steamboats. Such were the lives of Emma and Frank, as he came to be known, over the ensuing three years. I must tell you I'm getting close to the end of my story now, though I'll need to confer with my sources. And anyway it's your turn."

It was also time for them to leave Ubud. Márgara vacillated between a desire to remain, and her sense of duty to Camila. And then there was the temptation to just drop everything and travel to California like Francisco and Emma. David put those thoughts into words. "What if we just escape, Margarita?" he says while he kisses her breasts, moistening them with his tongue. He senses her tension and excitement, and seeks out her mouth with his. She doesn't quite hear the question at that moment, only later, sweaty, with their legs confused, does she remember it. Escape, to where? The world is wide, I can take you to Myanmar, or New York, if you prefer. Don't you have to go back to Cambodia? I should, but . . . the only thing I want at the moment is to be inside you, or like this, with your body clinging to mine. She is about to say yes, let's go, wherever you want, with your body clinging to mine. What about Camila? I don't know, Margarita, how can I know? But I don't understand how you can take responsibility for something that's not your business. And what is it exactly that you're waiting for in Cambodia? Is it your business?

He draws away to look into her eyes: as much mine as Camila is yours.

"David, let's be honest with one another. I can't leave because Camila's husband is in some kind of trouble. She says it's just financial, but who knows? The fact is that he sent for her, which I suppose means he's in hiding. I can't tell you anything more because I honestly don't know. Can I just leave her?"

"It depends on how capable she is of dealing with her own problems. She ought to be able to by now, or at least she should learn how. Maybe she doesn't learn because she knows you'll always be there."

"Actually it's the first time I've seen her this vulnerable. Camila's always been her own person. She's never needed me before."

"All right then. You'll see that I have infinite patience when it comes to waiting for you."

"Oh, well, isn't that a relief. Mr. Wonderful to the rescue! Here I am confessing a secret that's not even mine and you . . ." She's so indignant she can't even finish her sentence. She jumps up and wraps herself in the first thing she can find, the bedspread they threw upon the floor.

"That's quite a thing to say after a declaration of love," he tries to embrace her but Márgara pulls away.

"Quit joking around."

"Who's joking? Come on. I'm with you, let's be completely honest with one another. But in order for me to do that I need time—time when I'm not distracted looking at you in such an alluring outfit. Let's have dinner."

Dinner passes uncomfortably. He's chatty and full of light-hearted humor, though her replies are little more than monosyllables. At last they get up and go out strolling along the hotel's garden pathways. Eventually, David begins to speak.

"When my father died in 1970, I was fourteen years old. My brother and I were at school in the United States when my mother and her husband came to give us the news personally. My father's name was Stephen Masters (being an American citizen he dropped the 'Iturbe'), and he was a diplomat. We all went to the funeral in Washington. The assumption was that he'd died in Bangkok in the line of duty, and no one bothered to explain the circumstances to my brother and me. Since we weren't exactly close we just sort of let the matter drop. But in order to explain what I need to explain to you, I need to back up some and tell you what I found out about it. I realize that all I've been doing is telling you stories, but this is completely true and honestly not very pleasant. You didn't have to live it, and come to think of it I didn't either, but I've learned it piece by piece. It's the story of how some ruthless individuals in the 1969 White House destroyed a country. That is to say, President Richard Nixon and Henry Kissinger, who was Nixon's advisor first and only secondarily his Secretary of State. In March of that year they hatched a secret plan to bomb Cambodia, a neutral country and supposed ally of the United States in the war against the North Vietnamese. The objective, which was considered absurd by the majority of military strategists in the US (thus the need for secrecy), was to destroy sanctuaries in the Cambodian jungle that supplied the Vietcong. In other words, the famous Ho Chi Minh Trail, which started in China and snaked through the jungle through Laos and Cambodia and into Vietnam. I don't want to make this story too long, so let me just say that over the next fourteen months 3,630 missions were flown by American B-52's. They razed farms and villages, killing their inhabitants, without ever achieving their aim of destroying what they called the COSVN—the Central Office of South Vietnam. But the premise was ridiculous."

"But, how could the bombings be secret? Someone had to have known."

"Nixon and Kissinger knew, but not many others in Washington. Sure, some information was leaked, but at the time no one paid much attention. The system was Machiavellian anyway. Planes would take off under false orders and then be redirected over Cambodian territory. Military traffic coordinators had orders to burn any document related to the changes in coordinates. The whole thing infuriated a man by the name of Hal Knight, the major in charge of the operation, who ultimately made a declaration before Congress. Official records showed only legitimate military targets, if we can call them that, within the boundaries of Vietnam. The following year, Nixon maintained that the United States had scrupulously respected Cambodia's neutrality during the previous five years. But the end result of all that bombing was that they dispersed the North Vietnamese and their Khmer Rouge allies into the interior of Cambodia. That had the effect of destabilizing Prince Sihanouk's government, which then fell in a *coup d' état* to Lon Nol. That left the country in a state of near total anarchy, setting the stage for the 1970 ground invasion by the South Vietnamese and Americans in support of Lon Nol—their supposed new ally. When the news was finally made public in the US, the protests only intensified. Students died at the hands of the National Guard, creating an atmosphere of repression that in the end led to Watergate and Nixon's fall."

"Tell me the truth now David. Are you involved with the CIA or something like that?"

"Of course not. These aren't state secrets I'm telling you. It's all public information, though the public at large doesn't seem to be interested.

"So with Cambodia all but destroyed, submerged in chaos, it succumbed to the extremist movement of the Khmer Rouge. Pol Pot, as we talked about, tried to remove Cambodia from modern life, to transport it back to a utopian rural past, and in the process he murdered or exiled an indeterminate number of Cambodia's inhabitants. You saw some of the results on the way out of Angkor Wat: hundreds, thousands of mutilated people, a land sown with mines, a wrecked economy and an unstable government."

"It's all terrible and fascinating David, but I'm lost. How do you know so much? And what does your father have to do with it?"

"I know because I've spent years finding it all out. As for my father, I've been able to ascertain that he didn't die peacefully in his office in Bangkok, but rather flying over bombed-out zones in Cambodia, collecting information for his friends in Washington. Somehow he found out what was happening and wanted to expose it. What I still haven't found out, and maybe there's no point to it now, is whether it was an accident or if he was shot down. He was traveling with a North American reporter and two Cambodians."

"So what are you looking for then? The truth?"

"No, that's long lost, lost in the jungle. It's ancient history now. You were a baby then, I was a boy. No, I'm not interested in truth. There was a time, when I was younger, I was proud of the way he died. Now what I'm seeking, or rather hoping to find, is a person: my sister."

"I thought you said you had a brother."

"Well she's my half-sister, really. The daughter of my father and his Cambodian wife. She's the one who told me about the flight and something else I didn't know: about the person we actually buried in Washington. It wasn't my father. In fact they never found the remains of the accident, the plane or the bodies. They probably never even looked for them."

"I certainly understand your obsession with Cambodia now. It seemed so strange to me that you'd have traveled so much to a country stuck in permanent conflict. . . ."

"So you see there really are no mysteries. The first time I ever came here was with her, with Thary. I fell in love with this place. I wanted to find out more about what my father was looking for. It's strange, you know, in life he never was a real person to me. He traveled a lot, got involved with Thary's mother, divorced my mom (Thary is several years younger than I am) then got lost somewhere in Asia. He'd send us letters, gifts, or money on our birthdays and visit us from time to time, but he mostly just wasn't there. Yet there are people whose images persist in us, pictures not of who they really are but of who we wish they'd been. For me that image grew stronger all the time. That is, until I finally met my real father through what Thary told me about him. She of course didn't spend much time with him either. He died when she was just a girl. Yet the image of him that her mother projected was so strong. . . . It's funny, my brother couldn't give a damn about him. I don't know if I've made him larger than life by fixating on his final act."

"So that's why it's so easy for you to create my great-grandpa out of nothing."

"I suppose so. Though I think that it's time for me to stop making people up and start concentrating on the living."

"But you are here for a living person, aren't you. Your sister."

"Which I suppose means I'm not entirely crazy."

"That all depends. But I have another question. Why

all the mystery? And that cryptic thing you said about me loving you so much nothing would matter to me?"

"Well, is it true? Do you love me?"

"Don't change the subject, just answer."

"Seriously, Margarita, do you love me?"

She looks at him and smiles.

"I'm starting to consider it."

David's Story

With Márgara asleep beside him, David gets out of bed carefully. He opens the bar and takes out two little bottles of brandy, plus a few cigars so he doesn't have to bother fumbling with his cigarette case. He slides the door open and walks out onto the terrace. The moonless night just barely reveals the silhouettes of the hotel rooftops and the outline of the grove surrounding it. There is a light breeze, and the darkness hums with insects. It is a moment of perfect solitude. Even so, he doesn't feel the peace he usually does when he's so close to nature. Why all the mystery indeed? He's deliberately woven a web of mystery around himself. A tactic of seduction? Maybe at first, but not later. Márgara became too important. He enjoyed telling her about his father, about Cambodia. And Thary? How will you tell her story?

He met her at the university. It was his father's only enduring legacy: American university educations, which he provided for his children via a trust fund. Esteban decided to go north while David preferred the California climate, mostly for the sports: year-round tennis, long runs along the beach, bike rides on the coast. Academics just an excuse to keep up his lifestyle, and so he carried on studying publicity without any greater ambitions. One day he received a phone call from his mother informing him that he was about to be visited by a foreign girl. She'd just given her his address. She was nervous and became evasive when he insisted on knowing his visitor's identity. There was something strange in her voice. It's too late for me to explain it to you now, Thary will do it. It was the first time he'd heard her name and at that moment all he felt was slight annoyance at the prospect of entertaining a stranger. He soon forgot all about it. When a roommate came to the tennis court to tell him he had a visitor, he didn't even connect it to the phone call.

Thary with the golden skin. She stood there waiting for him in the visitor's lounge of his dormitory, a tourist in jeans and a backpack. She had jet black hair that reached down to her waist. Seeing how pretty she was, he was delighted his mother had thought of him. She smiled, approached and gave him a kiss. I'm so happy to finally meet my brother. He stared like at an alien that has just landed on the dining room table. He didn't utter a word. She cocked her head slightly and repeated in her honey-like voice: I'm very happy to meet you. The first thing that occurred to him was to tell her there had been a mistake. My name is David Masters-Iturbe, I don't have any sisters, you must be looking for someone else. Yes, you're David, your mother told me where to find you, didn't she tell you?

It took him hours to unravel the mystery, then months to forgive his mother for organizing such a get-together. Thary was his half-sister, and in keeping with family tradition, was about to begin her studies at a university in the US. She'd picked one based on its proximity to the brother she'd never met. From what he could gather, information had been flowing among the family, but only in one direction. This girl knew everything about him, his life, his studies, practically what he ate for breakfast this morning, while he hadn't even known she'd existed before a few moments ago. As soon as it was convenient he passed her off to someone who could help her get settled and went straight to the telephone. The first person he tried was Esteban, but with no luck. The next thing he heard was his mother's *hello*, more irritating than ever. He immediately started shouting, demanding some coherent explanation for what was happening. What came wasn't coherent, but it was an explanation. In retrospect it doesn't matter all that much. The important thing was: how to explain Thary? The facts were simple enough: name, date and place of birth, mother's maiden name (deceased). Yet it took quite an effort to assimilate the sudden acquisition of a sister. For her part, the new discovery didn't cause any conflict for Thary, probably because it wasn't new. He and his brother were evidently a frequent topic of conversation in his father's new family. At first he was furious to think that during the entire time he was being talked about (or acknowledged at any rate) no one had even bothered to tell him that his father had another wife and child. He promised when I was grown he would take me to meet you, Thary said, but then he died so soon after. It was then that he learned the actual circumstances of his father's death, in tones so admiring he began to wonder just who this man was who called himself his father, yet had been so distant.

David tells Márgara the whole story the following morning, making her laugh almost to tears with jokes about his mother's terminal case of discretion. In the course of the tale, he takes her on a tour of the old university gardens, introduces her to friends, and escorts her to football games. He actually speaks very little of Thary, which only makes Márgara more curious.

The most consequential mysteries are the inner ones, the ones we make up because we're afraid of reality. They pile up in layers of evasion, burying thoughts and emotions and creating a dark zone where strangers aren't allowed.

You can't conjure up Thary, the one from your memory, because you feel guilty. Guilty about what? You never said anything or did anything more than she allowed or invited. Which makes you guilty of cowardice, for not having given her the opportunity to decide for herself. Perhaps it was a game of misunderstanding and you both lost. Because you never saw the harm in loving her or wanting her. You never understood the conventions that dictate who you can love and how. If you hadn't known that she was your father's daughter, if she was just any other girl, would it have been different? It's forbidden to desire your sister. But then she isn't, even if you have the same father. You didn't grow up together, didn't establish the usual pattern of protection, competition, even resentment that puts up natural barriers in families. There's also the biological element of course, the necessity of continuing the species. It was no accident that royal lineages degenerated, that they eventually stopped procreating among themselves and began looking outward. But we're not talking about procreation. Loving, yes. You loved her madly and without telling her in words, because it was obvious. You loved her without guilt, though with the fear of one day seeing in her eyes a rejection of something she wanted but couldn't admit. How would such a circumstance be treated in the East? Would it be a taboo there as well? But then later the real guilt would have come, because you'd complicated her life, you'd put her in an unacceptable situation, when she looked to you, trusted you. There was Thary in your New York apartment, after you'd finished school. Hi David I'm here, I'm on vacation. I came to study at your house, I get too distracted back at school. She'd study for hours, curled up in his arms on the old gray sofa, while he amused himself with a book or the TV. All right, enough already, take me out dancing. All those nights of going to cafes and bars, clubs where he watched her dance with him, or with others. And why not, I'm here with my brother. (He never knew which was the worse torture.) Sometimes it would be: let's not go out tonight, I'll cook for you. She'd make him buy all the ingredients for the Thai or Chinese food that she liked: flavors that seemed strange to him at first and that later he longed for, perhaps because they brought to mind the brush of her hand while they did dishes, played cards, rolled around on the carpet. In one contentious game of poker he literally pulled an ace out of his sleeve, just a trick to make her laugh. Feigning indignation she flings down the cards, and playfully starts pulling hair and punching, until he loses his balance and they fall, chair and all, onto the floor. He feels her body on top of him, shaking with laughter, and in the struggle he's no longer touching clothing but naked skin. Thary's lips are so close to his he tries to kiss her. She makes a sudden movement and he finds his mouth pressed against her neck. A prisoner in his arms, she remains immobile, mute, until she breaks free at last. Excited and out of breath, he looks for a complicit glance in her eyes, some indication of reciprocal emotion. All he sees is her smoothing her hair, arranging her clothes and laughing at innocent games. Could she be that innocent or that blind? The scene made him aware of his own lack of control. Imagining her in the next room, in bed or walking about with tousled hair and sleep in her eyes, in a tight shirt, made his nights a torment. When Thary finally went back to the school, when only the echo of her voice was left in the apartment, he prescribed a treatment for himself that even now, so many years afterward, surprises him for its ingenuity. You were like a teenager in heat, chasing any female who crossed your path, most of whom were attracted to a passion that was merely anxiety in disguise. You tried to fall in love but failed every time. And in between, your long periods of isolation were punctuated by Thary's letters, irregular, some a mere three-line note, others a multi-page volume of breathless, uninterrupted scribbling. About that time, Mercy appeared. Her arrival coincided with Thary's internship (don't come and see me, I don't have a second free) and for the first time he felt liberated. Mercy's Latino roots, an ambiguous inheritance that they shared—created affinities, complicity in the Anglo world that surrounded them. He was about to tell Mercy about Thary, to put words around an increasingly serious relationship, when Thary called. I'm graduating in two weeks, I want you to come. Without even thinking he'd made his decision. He offered to take her on a trip. You need a vacation and I owe you a present. Let's go to Paris.

You'll have to tell her all of that. But then your mystery stopped being a mystery a while ago. If you don't mention it, if you assume that it never existed for anyone else but you, then everything becomes easy.

They eat and leave Ubud behind. She checks the room one last time to see if she's forgotten anything. She sees the terrace, the wooden shutters, and wants to take it all with her, to take the whole room so she can go back to it when she wants. David takes her suitcase and takes her by the hand. Come, we'll have many more like it.

Back in Bali she runs to the hotel desk to ask if any messages arrived for her. One phone call from Mrs. Camila Rendón. She'll call back. No, she didn't say where she was calling from.

"I put the room in your name, in case they called you. Or did you want your own?" David says with such a surprised expression it makes her laugh. "Oh what a relief, I thought for a moment we were going to go back to playing hide and seek."

"She called and I wasn't here to answer. I shouldn't have left here, David."

"You don't think you're going to run off like James Bond and save your brother-in-law's life, right? Besides, I don't think that there's much of anything you can do."

"I can be available at least."

"Being available is dangerous, Margarita. It cheapens a relationship."

"Look who's talking. You've done nothing but be available since I met you. It's practically your profession."

"That's different. I do it for the pleasure I get from giving you pleasure."

"What about your sister?"

"I do that out of affection, but don't anguish over it. Camila told you to wait a week, right? We were only gone for three days."

"It seems an eternity."

"It sure does. Important things have a way of stretching out time. Or shortening it, I don't know."

Waiting. Waiting again, but it's different this time with David at her side. Part of her wished for just some sign that Camila was okay, so she'd be free to wander the world without having to worry.

"I know why I'm here in Bali, what I have to do. You don't have to stay here."

"I already told you, you're the reason I'm here."

"Don't treat me like a child David, or some woman who you have to take care of."

"You don't believe I'm here because of you? Then why the hell would I spend so much time sitting on this beach when some of the most beautiful places on earth are just a stone's throw away?"

"So I'm supposed to feel guilty now?"

"Margarita, I wouldn't care if we were in the middle of the desert. I'm happy just being with you."

"Alright, I'm convinced. But that's not why you're here in the first place. You were in Angkor because you were waiting for something, no, someone, your sister. What happened?"

"I can wait here just as easily. It's the age of communications. But, you've got to be tired of hearing my stories by now. True, false, or otherwise. If I were stuck reading a novel where all a guy did was talk, I'd throw the thing out the window."

"I know I would, but this isn't a novel. And anyway I like your stories."

"All right then, come over here and get comfortable. I trust my pipe won't bother you. I'm going to finish up with Francisco now so you can get back to your story. So now. When we last left our heroes they were wandering the Wild West, cleaning up at the gambling tables. But now comes the drama. On arriving one day in Abilene, a town that was almost a city proper, Francisco and Emma settled down for a rest in their hotel room. They were bathing, or at least Francisco was bathing Emma in one of those old-fashioned iron tubs that's made to hold only one person. The lack of space gave Francisco the opportunity to soap up every inch of her body and trace designs in the foam on her breasts. She retaliated by throwing handfuls of suds back at him. Their little game was interrupted by Sam, who unceremoniously kicked open the door. Not even noticing the two of them were naked, he said breathlessly: Four-Aces Jack is in town, and he's telling everyone who'll listen that he's here to challenge the two of you to a duel at daybreak. Emma got up and wrapped herself in a sheet. Is there any way out of here? None, Sam said. He's got a man posted at every exit. Panicked, Francisco forgot they weren't even dressed. Take the horses to the outskirts of town, Sam, we'll slip away under cover of night. But Emma, putting her hand on his arm said: it's useless. The only thing we'd get for our trouble would be a bullet in the back in some alley. It's high time we faced him. Francisco's face turned a still lighter shade of pale. All right then, tell him I'll be there. Emma signaled for Sam to leave, took Francisco by the hand and sat him down on the bed. I'm the one who has to go, Francisco. I'm a better shot than you. He began to protest, but she gently put her fingers to his lips. I'm the one they want. If I do by some chance bring him down, they'll probably let us go. But if you throw down and hit him, his men will finish us for sure. That argument didn't make any sense at all to Francisco, who was adamant. But there was no way to convince her. Sam came back a short while later with her pistols, clean and loaded, and told him: Emma's right. Terrified and feeling like a dreadful coward, Francisco spent the worst night of his life in that bed. They rose before sunup and got dressed. Strapping on their guns, they headed down to the street to join Sam. They were surprised to see how many people had gathered. This is a circus, Francisco said, furious. It's better that way, Emma said. He'll have to fight fair in front of so many witnesses. The sight of the sheriff and two of his deputies on some nearby porch steps consoled him. As the appointed hour grew near, Emma walked slowly to the middle of the street. She drew her pistol, spun the cylinder two or three times and holstered it again. Francisco saw Four-Aces Jack emerge from the crowd looking like the devil himself, dressed all in black, his hat pulled down to his eyebrows, chaps dragging in the dusty street. At the other end of the street was Emma's fragile silhouette against the daybreak. The sight put a knot in his throat. This can't be happening, he thought to himself. He tried to dive headlong into the street but Sam held him back. Calm down, he said. The black man's eyes, nervous, scrutinized every nook and cranny of the scene. All eyes were fixed upon the hands of the clock in the church tower. When the minute hand grazed the hour, two shots rang out in unison. For a moment time stood still. The opponents faced each other. Then, suddenly, Emma's body bent and fell. Francisco let out wail. He broke free of Sam's grip and ran toward her, as did many from the crowd. It was his last moment of consciousness.

"What do you mean 'his last moment of consciousness'? He can't die."

"No one said he's dead. When he opened his eyes, amid shadows and dizziness, he saw the face of an Indian boy leaning over him. The boy helped him sit up, then forced open his lips and poured a bitter, scorching brew into his mouth. He was in some kind of conical tent. His head pounded, and when he went to touch his face he noticed his fingers were covered with dried blood. Gradually he began to remember: the duel, the shots, Emma's body . . . Emma! He leapt up and began shaking the boy. Emma! What happened to Emma?! But the boy just shook his head and said something in a strange language. He crawled out of the tent on all fours into the blinding sun where he heard the sound of voices and neighing horses. Around him was an Indian village. Women were sewing hides, children were playing. In desperation he began to shout in English, then in Spanish: Please! Is there anyone who can understand me here? They looked at him curiously though no one came near. Stumbling among the teepees he approached the women, the children. Please, someone, please help me. Finally the boy approached him, took him by the arm and led him into the largest of the village's tents. Still disoriented, it took him a while to distinguish two men in the darkness, crouching on hides, smoking long pipes. One of them gestured for Francisco to sit down, then put his fingers to his lips to indicate silence. Francisco, still extremely weak, let himself fall to the ground. The silence went on. Each time Francisco tried to speak, the man gestured once again for him to be quiet. When in desperation he finally got up to leave, the older man held him down. He took the pipe from his mouth and said in broken Spanish: I have a message for you, *kemosabe*. Then he held out a set of saddlebags that Francisco recognized immediately. How? Those are mine, where . . . ? The Indian looked at him reproachfully, then gestured for Francisco to open them. They were overflowing with bills. On a stained piece of paper a note read: She's not here any more. Go home. Sam.

"Francisco spent weeks, months among the Indians. Lying delirious on the floor of his wigwam, he tossed and turned, called to Emma, even Sam. Sometimes, between his fevered dreams, he'd glimpse the boy's face, other times he'd see a very old Indian woman leaning over him, murmuring a monotonous litany. As time passed he was able to stand and leave the tent. Such was his weakened conditioned that he'd remain sitting outdoors for hours, watching the comings and goings of the villagers and the children at play. One day a man approached him, the same man who'd given him the saddlebags, and said: winter is coming and we are leaving. It is better for you to go back to your own land. Francisco tried to thank him by giving him one of the saddlebags. For the boy who took care of me, for the woman, he said. The old Indian just shook his head and pointed to the plains. Shortly the boy brought a horse that he recognized as his old mount, Gunshot, fat from pasturing and doing next to nothing. Another boy, just a child, appeared by his side to guide him. The last thing he saw of the village was the silhouette of the old man with his arm raised high. Behind him the rising smoke of campfires. They rode for almost two days. At dusk on the second day, the young guide pointed to some lights in the distance. Mohawk, he said, then turned and galloped away.

"Being right back where he started seemed like a cruel joke to Francisco. When he entered the saloon he thought that he was dreaming. Right there at a table was Guzmán, who stared at him without recognition. Don't you know me Guzmán? I'm Francisco Videgaray. The fellow looked at him again, squinting his eyes, then suddenly got up and embraced him. I told you that every road leads to the same place around here. And so Francisco went home, skinnier, though considerably richer, and with a beard and a touch of gray in his hair that made him look quite a bit older. So. Now you tell me how he met your great-grandma, making it possible for you to be here with me now."

"Oh I can't. After an odyssey like that, my part of the story is just a silly soap opera."

"After my cheesy story?"

"What are you talking about? You even told it live and in Technicolor. You picked the wrong profession you know. You should have been a writer."

"I was always tempted. But all I know how to do is mix up the things I already know, like ingredients in a cocktail shaker. But one thing is true: I have a good memory. I could tell you the name of the movie that each one of those scenes comes from."

Francisco, the redskins, and a dead woman lying in the middle of a dusty street all swirled around in Márgara's head. But there was no denying that the central image was a man whose life had been decimated by the loss of his love. He's telling her his own life story, populated by cowboys and gamblers. It's true he certainly has the look of a man who's lived through tragedy. When Francisco married my great-grandma, did he feel Emma's body every time he made love to her? Oh, you're such an idiot, Márgara. No one knows what Francisco Videgaray did in the years he was away. But does he feel the body of another woman when he makes love to you? Oh that's madness. The only sane person in the room is the man sleeping next to you, who turns your world on its head with his stories. And with his being. You're done telling stories. Let Francisco go on living in love with his Emma. Let no woman take her place. Great-grandma, like a shadow, is superimposed on Camila, and, you realize with a shiver, on you as well.

The phone rang early: I'll be there this afternoon.

"Camila?" David asked, half awake.

"Yes, she's coming today."

"I'll leave you two alone. Anyway I have to go to Phnom Penh for a few days. I need to see someone."

"It doesn't matter what Camila decides, David. I'm going back to Mexico."

"You're not going to wait for me?

"I don't plan on waiting for anyone ever again."

"I thought you liked waiting with me."

"Don't you see? The two of you, for entirely different reasons, are anchored to this place. I don't have anything to do here."

"Didn't you just say you needed to support your sister? Personally, I'd like to think you've invested something of yourself these last few days. Am I mistaken?"

"No, but . . . I'm not Camila."

"Which one?"

"Neither."

"I know that. And I know you have to take care of your investments, Margarita. Do you think I'm going to evaporate on my way to Phnom Penh? I want to leave you two alone for a little while, not be a nuisance. I'll be back in three days and then you can decide what you want to do."

"You know I feel like one of those palm trees? Rooted down with the wind battering me from all sides."

"A very beautiful palm tree, though I'd never have thought to make the comparison."

My loyal sister. Camila embraces her and asks the porter to bring her suitcase up to her room. Hanging her raincoat in the closet, she notices a jacket and some shoes belonging to David. She raises her eyebrows in mute questioning.

"He went to Cambodia."

"Forever?"

"No, to give us some time alone."

"Is he as good in bed as he is out of it?"

"You mean you don't know?"

"No."

"I thought that the night in Angkor, when you didn't come back. . . ."

It was the night Márgara had gotten so angry with Camila for peppering David with questions. She'd left them alone. And so without a witness Camila pressed him for more answers. But in the end he didn't give her any more information and still retained his sense of humor. You probably don't feel comfortable talking in public, she told him. Want to invite me up to your room for a drink? He got up, signed the bill, took her by the arm and walked her silently back to his room. It was more spacious than theirs, with a small adjoining living room (perhaps because he's a regular customer?). It was in perfect order, except for the desk, where his laptop sat, lost amid a mountain of paper. David turns on the dresser light and takes his jacket off. What kind of drink do you have in mind to make me talkative? She sits down on the sofa, lights a cigarette and stares at him. He offers her a tall whisky with a slightly shaky hand, the ice clinks in the glass. Camila brushes his fingers as she takes the glass from his hand and tries out her famous gaze, upward, through her eyelashes. Still, he doesn't sit down beside her, rather he pushes his computer aside and sits down on the desktop. He looks down at her from his vantage point, a half-smile on his face that she doesn't know how to interpret. Her interrogation has lost all momentum and the silence starts to get uncomfortable. Perhaps to break it, David rummages through his papers and hands her an envelope: pictures from the other day. Do you want to see them? Camila quickly flips through the stack until she gets to the one of the three of them at Ta Prohm. She shows it to him: what a clever camera you have, it takes pictures by itself. Giving the photo to him, she leaves her hand on his. David frees himself so he can look more closely at the picture, but seeing Camila's hand in the air he takes it once again. We'll have to show them to Márgara tomorrow, she must already be asleep. Camila regards him for a moment, then rises impatiently, puts the glass down on the desktop and gives him back the envelope. Yes. Tomorrow. Definitely. But it's late now. David shows her to the door, and wraps her in the shawl she took off when she arrived. He takes her by the shoulders, turns her toward him and gives her a light kiss on the lips. Good night.

"It hurts my pride a little to say so, but no. You're the one he wanted from the start. Happy?"

"Yes and no."

"Oh take a stand for once, Márgara. He's a fabulous guy."

"Well, yes, but I don't know. There are some things . . ."

"Oh, you never know what you want."

"You, on the other hand, always know. And what good has it done you?"

"I didn't know what I wanted from David, but at least I'm not living in constant limbo."

"Which I suppose means you're staying with Bobby?"

"Right. I just came back for my things while he puts everything in order. He's going to call me in a few days so I can meet up with him."

"Where?"

"I'll write to you in Mexico, Márgara. Assuming you're going back."

"You can be sure about that."

"What about David?"

"I have no idea what he's going to do, but I know what I'm going to do. But please tell me if you'll be okay with Bobby."

"Don't worry about me. Say what you will, he knows how to take care of me. And things will work out, you'll see. We'll show up in Mexico when you least expect it."

The Phnom Penh he finds waiting for him is not the one from years gone by. When Márgara talked about her fascination with Cambodia, an intrigue born of shadowy hallways and rays of light illuminating the Khmer smile, he could see himself in that museum. He'd had a similar feeling. The desire to go, to see those faces up close. Thary saw it in him. She threw her arms around his neck: you have to come with me. But it took them years to get there. By then, Thary had finished her postgraduate work and was a member of Doctors Without Borders. But on that day, dazzled by visions of a utopian Cambodia, he takes her to lunch with the intention of proposing something that no longer seems like madness. Stay with me, we'll go far away, where no one knows us and we can make a life together. He orders a bottle of champagne and raises a glass to her brand-new degree, to the trip they're on, to the circumstances that allowed them to meet, so long ago. You are the finest inheritance my father could have left me: my brother, she says, all sentimental, her eyes glistening. The word unsettles him. He leaves his glass on the tabletop since the shaking of his hands threatens to spill the drink. I have something to tell you Thary. I have something to tell you too, she says. I wanted you to be the first to know: I'm getting married, to a colleague, a doctor. We've made big plans and I want to tell you all about them. David remembered nothing after that.

He was the most affectionate best man possible, as well as the most supportive brother when the jeep Francis was traveling in crashed and Thary was left a widow so young. All through those years he'd managed to convince himself it had all been a dream, that he'd never been within a few words of proposing to his sister. It was only much later, when they finally made the trip to Cambodia, that he saw himself for what he really was and put his love for Thary in a new context.

They'd planned the trip several times over the years and cancelled it for a variety of reasons: she was on a mission, David and Esteban were taking over the paper company (an inheritance from their step-father). But then one day, a day just like today, he found himself on a plane. It had taken him a long time to get a visa from a country with very few embassies and very little sympathy for Americans. Phnom Penh seemed a sad city, despite all the traffic (a swirl of motorcycles, bicycles and very few cars) and the atmosphere of the Heart of Darkness, a bar patronized by forms of life common to such places: journalists, members of volunteer organizations, the UN. Thary is accustomed to the environment and tries to include him. Still, he feels left out. The trucks full of Vietnamese soldiers with their AK-47s and M-16s. The feeling of being in an occupied land. The visit to the Killing Fields with its mountains of skulls, testimony to Pol Pot's massacres. All these things confuse him. Back at the hotel, the receptionist leads them with great ceremony to the dining room, where they are the only diners. He tries to appreciate his half pineapple filled with rice and dried meat, and garnished with raisins that remind him of insects (he tries desperately to put the thought of flies out of his head). A friend of Thary's comes and takes them to the museum where bats, alarmed by their entry, flutter around their heads. He doesn't quite manage to find enchantment in the sculptures. Their smiles seem ironic in this atmosphere of abandon. They finish their tour by wandering along a dirt road at dusk. Emaciated girls, no more than twelve or thirteen, lean against the doors of their shanties, the bags under their eyes covered with masks of make-up. This is the red light district, explains their guide. Just then he would have boarded a plane to anywhere. Thary was all that kept him there.

Finally, they board a boat to Siem Reap. On the pier, the lame and mutilated beggars move him in the same way they did Márgara, so many years later. As they begin to negotiate the river, Cambodia starts working its magic. The fishermen on the shores, the verdure. There's a moment of fear when an army barge briefly detains them:

the uniforms, the guns, a language he doesn't understand, he and Thary crouching amongst the cargo so as not to provoke an incident. But when they arrive at the lake, he forgets everything. There is no horizon, nor sky, nor water. The boat slips soundlessly along, and they're suspended in the void. A few delicate poles emerge from the surface in rows, as though they'd been nailed there. They're all that recall order and physical laws. The rest is colorless, motionless. He and Thary are the only passengers who disembark in Siem Reap. This is his first adventure and he feels at a disadvantage. Thary lives and works in conflict zones, among the refugees, the persecuted, and so is immune to the sensation of not being welcome, of being an intruder who doesn't understand a thing that's going on. It is suffocatingly hot. There's no place to buy a cold drink or bottle of water—not that it even existed back then, at least in the way we think of it, as a symbol of globalization—and, after the magic of lake Tonle Sap, the town dispirits him. Spontaneously, inevitably, a guide appears. A very young boy, whom he rejects at first. Thary starts talking to him. She shows the young man a map and they work out itineraries and, presumably, payment. He takes them to a kind of enclosure topped with a palm roof, under which are several wooden tables. The owner tries to impress his unexpected guests, bringing them a pineapple similar to the one at the hotel in Phnom Penh. I'd just as soon die of hunger rather than eat another one of these, he thinks. Then the owner brings out something special, a dusty coca-cola. Every so often they hear the sound of passing vehicles, trucks with UN insignia on the side, or army jeeps.

That's the day he sees Angkor for the first time . . . *the city of the King of Twenty Kings.*

Seeing the surprise in Márgara's eyes made him remember his own from all those years ago. The difference being that on that day the place was deserted. Just the two of them and their guide, whose presence they soon forgot. Two monks in orange tunics appeared around a bend in a corridor, giving only slight acknowledgement and making no attempt to draw near. In Angkor Thom they met a UN doctor and his family—two girls who loitered beneath the watchful eyes of their mother. The man was on a mission in Phnom Penh and had come to spend the day. He took David by the arm and led him away to warn him about mines. Don't go off the paths or explore solitary places. Deserters sometimes hide around here. David thanked him for the advice, though he wanted to ask him what exactly he meant by solitary, since apart from these chance encounters, the place seemed to exist solely for them. Ta Prom left him speechless. He was reminded of some words by Kipling, though at the time he was unable to place the author. He reread various books afterwards, in an attempt to find them. When he finally did he copied them down and carried them in his wallet, like a talisman, a symbol of a kind of magic that can enter one's life. A sense of magic and of darkness was what Ta Prom offered him. Fascinated by a tangle of giant roots that seemed to have merged with the temple's stone wall, he wandered away from Thary and the guide. He was struggling to tear his gaze away so he could pay attention to the uneven floor when he felt, more than saw, someone standing nearby. Like a jungle spirit emerging from the trunk of a ceiba tree was a man dressed all in black, watching them from a narrow outcropping. He had a red-checkered kerchief around his neck and a gun in his hand. David remained motionless, not threatened physically, but rather possessed by some all-encompassing fear, as though he were being confronted by a warning that had been made flesh in a man. He attempted a greeting, some sign of recognition between two people alone in the world. But the soldier (a deserter? a guard?) didn't respond so David slowly drew away. He found Thary shortly after, and she signaled to him to listen. It took him a few moments before he could bring his rapid breathing under control and distinguish the sound. There were notes coming from some place behind a wall, a melody that faded at times only to reemerge, gently. Thary took him by the hand and led him to a spot where they could see. Not far away, seated on the fragment of a column, a girl was playing an instrument, a small flute. Her feet were bare and her hair was in disarray: a Pan come to enchant the lands of the king of twenty kings. He's come back to Angkor enough times now to confuse his various memories, but he always carries that first impression with him. Thary and Cambodia are joined like the roots of a ceiba to the walls of Ta Prom. To think of one is to think of the other; the times he was there with her, both good and bad. . . .

Now he's going to make one last attempt to contact her. Part of his reluctance to talk about her to Márgara was simple precaution: she was a stranger. Thary has, has always had, dangerous political connections in this unstable country. Perhaps it was the memory of her father that led her down a road of secrets, of incursions into forbidden places. Doctors Without Borders aren't always welcome in the countries they visit, despite the humanitarian work they do. They smell of foreignness, of interference. One of the reasons for his trips to Cambodia had been to make sure she was safe, to see her, convince her to come back with him. So she would at least know he was available. A friend told him that she's in a camp on the border with Thailand, the kind they used to set up to take care of refugees during wartime. Nowadays they're mostly dismantled, but there are always refugees, certainly from misery if not from bullets. Someone involved in the simple task of helping others shouldn't be so hard to locate. For that reason he doubts the veracity of the information. Who knows what his beautiful sister is doing, what groups she's gotten herself involved with. Oh, how clandestine her life is, and how precarious her safety. This is his last attempt. He's already made so many, all of them fruitless. If Thary wants to emulate her father and die forgotten in some distant jungle, there's nothing more he can do. And maybe he shouldn't. He has a life to lead, outside of his never-ending pursuit of his sister and his attempts to save her when she doesn't want to be saved. Besides, now there is Márgara. Were you pursuing Thary for Thary's sake or for yours? When you think 'now there is Márgara' it means that something has changed.

"What a shame that there isn't a piano so we can live out that scene again. It would be the perfect *déjà vu*." He's come up from behind, surprising them. It's already evening at the bar beside the pool. The turquoise light of the water illuminates their faces. He kisses Márgara. Camila beckons him over to kiss him too.

"Well, well . . . the Flying Dutchman. You kidnapped my sister while I was gone. You know you can't trust anyone anymore?"

"How are you, Camila?"

"Don't even ask me. Tell us though, for starters, what you went to Phnom Penh for."

"Margarita?" David takes Márgara's hand and holds it over his lips.

"Wow, you even changed her name. And I'm not hearing any complaints."

Márgara silently caresses David's face. This isn't possible. Seeing him, you have no idea what you're going to say. She offers him her glass to buy a little time. David asks a neighboring table for a chair, places it beside Márgara, very close, and puts his arm around her shoulders.

"I went to look for a friend. He'd promised to find out where my sister is."

"And?"

"He didn't. They tell me she'll be back in a week or two. I'll call him from somewhere. What about you, Camila?"

"I said don't ask. I'm sure Márgara already explained it all to you anyway."

"How long are you staying?"

"No idea. A few days maybe. But look, now that we all know everything about each other and there are no mysteries anymore, why don't we just have a good time? We'll pretend that no one has to leave, that we're all back at the Grand Hotel and time is standing still. We're visiting temples and telling stories."

"Tomorrow maybe. For now let's get some sleep. Are you coming, Margarita?"

Camila feels her sister's hand squeeze her shoulder, then watches them walk off toward the rooms.

"Come by and get your toothbrush at least!" she shouts as they leave, then orders another drink.

David suggests they rent a car again and head up to the mountains, but Márgara won't agree to it. Camila has to wait for a phone call, so we can't leave. You go, David, wherever it is you have to go. It's not fair of me to keep you here.

"Now that's the worst *déjà vu* yet. You have to wait, I have to wait, we all have to wait. For eternity. Except no one's had to wait for you yet, which I guess makes you the hero."

"It's the last time I'm waiting for anybody."

"So we're back to threats now? I promise you'll never have to wait for anything ever again unless you want to. You certainly won't have to wait on my account. From here on in I'll follow after you. It's the most appealing occupation I can think of."

Camila is sunbathing. Her mouth, bright red with lipstick, peeks out from under her black sunglasses and a straw hat. Every so often she leans over to reach her vodka tonic. "Aren't you going to entertain me? What happened to David's story?"

"Are you ever behind," says David. "I finished my story a long time ago. It's all up to you two now."

"In your version, great-grandma loses the romantic halo we'd always put on her," Márgara says. "She's nothing but a hapless victim,"

"Oh, you've got it all wrong," David says. "There are no victims or guilty parties most of the time. Just misunderstandings caused by differing perspectives. It's my belief that people act according to their own viewpoints, without necessarily noticing those of others. Besides, you're forgetting that the facts may be very different from the way I imagined it. For all I know, Francisco's life was useless and boring and your great-grandma was his salvation."

"I'll tell you what happened," Camila says. "Great-grandma found her long-lost lover by sheer coincidence. They hooked up right away and got married. Later everything got all fucked up, but in the end she got what she wanted. But it's a pretty boring story." Camila yawns and covers her face with her hat.

"What, that's all?"

"Not quite," Márgara says. "It's true she found him by accident. She was off buying buttons or something. But whatever the case, it was a lovely morning and she'd decided to stroll along the Alameda. She stopped to watch some children playing in a fountain. After a moment she noticed a bearded man in the distance, also watching the children and smiling. She didn't recognize him at first. After so many years he looked very different from the young man at the wedding. Yet something in his eyes and smile caught her attention. And since he was distracted she was able to observe him at her leisure. Just then Francisco took out a cigar and lit it. That picture, of him tilting his head to the side to reach a flame, reminded her of a garden, of running to get there on time, and of a young man leaning against a railing with a cigar in his mouth. That image was so deeply etched in her mind that the real person, now standing almost directly in front of her, seemed like an illusion. Yet her wild heartbeat and breathlessness told otherwise. In an act of bravery that later seemed hard for her to believe, she walked around the children, right up to him and asked: Are you Francisco Videgaray? For his part he saw a beautiful and elegant woman standing before him (the years had passed here too, of course) and answered: Yes, miss. Somehow she had the presence of mind to give him the look (upward, through her eyelashes) and whisper: I am Camila Fuentes Ogarrio. Do you not remember me? We all know what effect that gaze has on men, and so there began—or rather continued—their relationship.

"I told you, she just hooked up with him and got married," Camila says. "And the family had plenty to say, I can tell you that. In fact, they almost disowned her."

“They got married against the will of the Ogarrio family,” Márgara says. “Just imagine, their only daughter and a man of questionable character, who'd been off for years doing who knows what. But then I suppose we do know now, thanks to you.”

“I don't *know*. I make up,” says David.

“So did the Videgarays,” says Márgara. “Taken as they were with Francisco's bride, they invented a trip, something between a study abroad program and a voyage of exploration. They made him into a virtual Livingstone, or better yet a Lord Byron. They were sure that Camila would be the salvation for such a good-for-nothing. But that didn't convince Desiderio, who didn't believe a word of what they said. He remembered all too well the rumors of cheating at cards, which he'd combined with other imagined offenses to create a nefarious character all too capable of taking advantage of his daughter's innocence. But then you have to remember that the girl was over twenty, a dangerous age in those days. That more than anything prompted Belén to back the whole thing. That or perhaps the fact that her future son-in-law had gotten even better looking, and exuded an air of maturity, though admittedly one which outstripped his abilities, both as a husband and a provider.

“Let's just say provider,” Camila says. “He must have been a terrific husband. Great-grandma was crazy about him.”

“Well they say she was crazy about him,” Márgara says. “That was true when he was around at least. That part of the story is vague. Families love to talk all about romantic details, but clam up where there's scandal afoot. Great-grandma's single life is a legend, but when she gets married her face just seems to disappear, as though it had faded from a mirror.”

"I'll tell you what happened," Camila says, sitting up. She orders another vodka tonic and pushes her hat back. "This whole idea of being a 'poor provider' is relative. Somehow or other he got hold of plenty of money, and they say it lasted them a good long while. They fell on hard times later. That's when papa Desiderio told Francisco he might be able to use his connections to get him a job or a business loan. Since his daughter was married to the guy he felt he had to do something. But Francisco wasn't the 9-to-5 type. All puffed up with pride he said he didn't want to owe anybody. My guess, though of course no one would ever have said this, is that Desiderio was tempted to simply make the bum disappear, but he wasn't about to leave his girl a widow. Divorce wasn't an option. But then later, as if by magic, things got better. The Videgarays for some reason gave him his inheritance in advance, which kept him quiet and out of trouble. Grandmother says he was the most charming man in the world. He loved his wife, his mother-in-law, and of course any member of the opposite sex, who were attracted to him like flies. He even ended up winning his father-in-law over in the end, probably because he never even looked at a deck of cards after that. The love he'd had for gambling turned to disgust. So he put all of his money—whether his own or someone else's, into making his woman happy. Such a nincompoop. But I guess she earned it after waiting all those years, with no guarantee he'd ever be back. And now here comes the mystery. Great-grandma got pregnant. It took a while, but she did. And that was what was peculiar, because there was no such thing as birth control back then. Women popped out children like rabbits. So everyone was jumping for joy when it happened. They even say Francisco reconsidered the job thing. At least until he finally showed his true colors and . . ."

"I'll take it from here," Márgara interrupts. "Because this part really is a mystery. Not only did Francisco give up, he changed. He went from being sunny and optimistic to sullen and distant. Worst of all he went back to gambling, but not for the sheer joy of winning like before. He didn't even attempt his old tricks. It's a sad chapter in the family history. He'd play for hours, concentrating, deaf to the world. Then one day he announced to great-grandma that he had to leave on an urgent trip. He promised to return in time for the baby's birth, packed a few things and disappeared. No one—literally no one, not even great-grandma or the Videgarays—ever heard from him again. Even now when she runs into a relative, my grandmother makes inquiries, just out of curiosity. The relatives, usually the nephews and nieces, remember having heard of great-uncle Francisco, but no one knows what happened to him.

"Imagine what a scandal that was. The very idea of a trip was suspicious. Francisco didn't have any business anywhere on the planet. Think of the humiliation for the Fuentes Ogarrio family, for their grandson—my grandfather Dante—to be born without a father. As far as they were concerned he had never existed at all. It was such a blow that they never spoke to the Videgarays again, or let them see the little boy. That's why Grandma Susan keeps looking into it when she runs into anyone from the family, to see if they know something. She'd love to be the one to discover the secret after all these years. But she'd better hurry up. Anyone who knows anything is getting on in years."

David looks at the two of them, pensive. After a while he calls the waiter over to order more drinks.

"There isn't any mystery," he says. "Not for the initiated, anyway. My source knows something you don't.

For the inexplicable change you mentioned just happened to coincide with the appearance of an exotic character at the Videgaray hacienda. He showed up one day, out of thin air, asking for Francisco. They told him that he didn't live there anymore and gave him his address in the capital. The man asked how he could get there on foot. When they told him how far it was he nodded, hoisted his haversack over his shoulder and ambled down the tree-lined path. It was some time later, no one knows exactly how much later, that a servant entered the dining room of Francisco's house and announced that a foreigner was looking for him. He went to greet the visitor, then shortly retreated with him to the study, where they locked themselves in. Curious, Camila questioned the servant. He's a strange man, ma'am, very large and very black. Determined to meet him she walked to the study where she found Francisco alone, pale, a letter in his hand. She'd never seen such a look on her husband's face before.

Rapt, they waited for David to continue, "Go on, tell us what happened!"

"Soon after came the transformation and ultimately the disappearance," David says. "Imagine what it must have been like. There he is, with a woman he loves, a child on the way and suddenly he's faced with this kind of dilemma?"

"Wait, I don't get it," says Camila. "What dilemma?"

"You missed the Masters-Iturbe version, sister," says Márgara. "A clever little turn of the screw by our friend David here. I can't decide if he is an incurable romantic or a cynic." Her tone betrays mild irritation.

"It's not romanticism, nor that other little ugliness you're suggesting," Davis says. "Don't underestimate the power of the great love stories, Margarita."

"I promise you I won't," Márgara says.

"You two are speaking in Sanskrit and I'm sick of the sun," says Camila. "Let's get dressed for dinner."

The days stretch out lazily in the sun. The Bali Sea is simple, just a blue, wet surface that doesn't excite travelers much, especially the ones accustomed to the turquoise of the Caribbean or the indigo of the Pacific coast. They take early runs on the beach, walk, read. Stories about the past are over, and the stories of the present are on hold. Camila is in an unusual situation, at least for her: she's a third wheel. At times she flirts with David like before. And if it weren't for David, for the way he responds to it, it would bother me. That's just Camila. No one talks about the future until Camila gets the call, the one that will put an end to this period of inertia.

"Bobby called last night," Camila says. "I have to meet up with him in three days. There's no need for you to wait with me here, Márgara. You two go wherever you want. You've done enough already."

"Are you sure?" Márgara asks.

"It's not fair of me to tie you down here," Camila says.

"I don't mean that," Márgara says. "Are you sure you want to go with Bobby? Or rather, is he sure you should go?"

"If he weren't he wouldn't ask me," Camila says. "But tell me honestly David, do you think I'm crazy too?"

"Of course not," David says. "I have no reason at all to think that."

"Oh now," Camila says. "I'm sure Márgara has supplied you with a few."

"She hasn't," David says. "She worries about you, that's as much as I've gotten."

"Do you think she has reason to?" Camila asks.

"Possibly," David says. "But really I'm in no position to judge."

"Oh cut the crap," Camila says. "I know she told you everything. But it's okay, it doesn't bother me."

"All I can tell you is what I told her." David says. "You're an adult, which means you're capable of deciding for yourself what's good for you."

"What she wants, maybe," Márgara says. "I'm not so sure she can decide what's good for her."

"You never change, Márgara," Camila says. "You can never stop judging everything I do."

"I don't think Márgara is making a judgment," David says. "Distance gives you a better perspective on some things."

"So now you're going to treat me like an idiot too?" Camila asks.

"You started this whole conversation," Márgara says, furious. "If you don't want opinions then don't ask."

"I feel like I'm at my own wake is all," Camila says. "Or that I'm a death row inmate and you're the priests walking me to the electric chair."

"I have no idea what you're condemning yourself to," Márgara says. "I certainly hope it's not death."

"I'm just doing what I feel like," Márgara. "And I feel like being with Bobby."

"And you have every right to want that, Camila," David says, suddenly trying to make peace. "As long as you know what it is you're getting into."

"Yes I know that," Camila says. "What Márgara doesn't understand is that someone can be one way with their partner and another way with everyone else. All that matters to me is the way he is with me, which happens to make me happy. But my sister here thinks I'm some kind of sheep who'll let herself be led to slaughter."

"All this talk of dead people and slaughterhouses is so overblown," David says. "Go be with your husband, Camila, and if something happens, you know you always have a family, and a country to go back to when you want."

"The voice of masculine wisdom," Márgara says. The tone is so hostile that it stops the conversation instantly. Camila moves silently away.

"I think that you already put your two cents in," David says. "Let her go in peace. But don't take it out on me."

"You're just Mr. Understanding aren't you David?" Márgara says. "You take her side when you know damned well how crazy this is."

"I'm not on anyone's side," Davis says. "And besides, it doesn't seem all that crazy to me."

"You don't know Bobby."

"No, I don't," he admits. "But I have to think she does. But the reality is that there's nothing you can do other than be there for her if she needs you." He draws her close to him and holds her for a long time.

I'm angry at Camila, I'm angry at David. I'm angry at myself. Camila and her realities. David and his stories. And where exactly do you fall, Margarita, between a reality and a story? She makes a phone call to reserve an airline ticket, then goes off to find her sister. She finds Camila in her room repeating a scene she's already witnessed: the robe, the hair pulled back, the cream being rubbed on her face. Márgara approaches her from behind and hugs her.

"Forgive me," Márgara says. "I hope everything works out just fine for you."

"You're an idiot, Márgara," Camila says. "Forget about me. Focus on David. Go with him—to Timbuktu if you have to, wherever his quest for that sister of his takes you."

"I'm leaving tomorrow," Márgara says. "And I'm not telling you where because you'll tell David. As far you're concerned I should follow him to the ends of the earth."

"I would," Camila says. "And would have if you hadn't beat me to him."

"Some nerve you have," Márgara says. "But I don't want to talk about it. So take care, please. Mother will know where I am if you need me."

"I can't for the life of me figure out why you're doing this," Camila says. "To fuck him over, I suppose. To get even? But you know what? I'm not at all worried about it. He's even more stubborn than you are and a lot more patient. And anyway, tonight I'll make my escape. I'll order dinner so you two can be alone. Tell him you're leaving, see what he says."

Tell him that you're leaving. See what he says.

They go out for a walk on the beach. The calm sea reflects the hotel lights. Water laps at the sand with a barely perceptible burbling. David takes his shoes off, ties the laces together and hangs them from his shoulder. He walks in a straight line, sinking down to his ankles and leaving footprints that turn into little pools. Also barefoot, she holds his hand with her left hand, and with the right Márgara holds up the edge of her long dress. But even so the water rises up to meet it, making it float for a moment. They walk all the way to where rocks block their path, creating a precarious refuge. The tide has left a high water mark on the stone. Facing her, David tries to loosen the knot that's holding her dress onto her shoulders, and ends up taking it off her completely. She feels the brush of dampened cloth and his gaze sweep across her naked body before he embraces her and lets himself fall upon her. This is a bad idea, Margarita, he says. You'll get covered with sand. We'll jump in the sea afterwards.

Her dress sticks to her wet body. Feeling her shiver, he wraps his shirt around her shoulders, then pulls her down on the rocks which are still warm from the afternoon sun. David, I'm leaving tomorrow.

"I'd hoped to be able to tell you that I'd be going with you, but then they called me . . ."

"It doesn't matter . . ."

"No listen to me first. I think I know where Thary is. It's the first information I've gotten that seems even remotely credible. But I can't take you—assuming you'd even want to come—and I'd have to be cracked to ask you to wait for me. But successful or not, the trip will be over in a couple of days. I'll catch up to you."

"I don't want to sit around and wait to see if you get lost in the jungle with your sister. She's the reason you're here. You've spent days and weeks waiting for news, so it must be very important, so much so you're willing to put your entire life on hold to find her. You and I are just something that happened in the interlude."

"It is important, in a way that's difficult for me to explain. When there's a presence in your life that's suddenly taken away, that person becomes an empty silhouette to you, like a sketch drawn on air. I'm determined to find her and convince her to leave this country. She's in danger here. Call it a debt I owe her. Unfinished business, you know? Like the movie. Anyway I'm the only one who can help her. She doesn't have anybody else as far as I know."

"Fine, good. But don't you see, I'm not about to underestimate the power of the great love stories, David.

I don't intend to meet up with you by chance a few years down the line."

"You aren't going to meet up with me by chance. I'm going to find you, wherever you are. That's the part you don't understand about love stories. Tell me where you're going."

"No."

"Then give me a month. Tell me where you'll be for the next month. If I don't manage to find Thary in that time then that's it. I'll have tried. No blame, no regrets. That part of my life will simply be over."

"And you'll spend the rest of your life thinking you didn't do enough."

"You don't know me, Margarita."

"That's what I'm afraid of."

He is awakened by the gentle sound of drawers, then water in the sink. He watches Márgara leave the bathroom in a robe, then dry her hair with a towel. Her suitcase is already packed and waiting beside the door. Come here: he stretches his arm out toward her. Márgara takes his hand and sits down beside him on the bed. Were you really thinking of leaving without saying goodbye?

"Of course I wasn't. I just didn't see why you should have to wake up at dawn too. I still have to do my hair. Let's order some breakfast."

"I'll take you to the airport."

"No."

"You're an incredibly stubborn woman. I can always ask at the desk you know, or ask the taxi driver. You won't be able to hide behind some phony address or disappear on some endless trip."

"I'm not going to hide."

He kisses her damp hair, then lightly pinches the tip of her nose between his fingers and shakes it.

"Relax, Margarita. Let's not argue now. You're sending me on an errant knight's quest. A month from now, probably on some Tuesday just like today, you'll see me walk through your door. After that point, I don't intend to leave again, ever. Well, okay, to go to work. This is an aspect of my personality you'll get to know in time."

In the airport the two women are surrounded by the usual crowd: sophisticates who fly as a matter of course, neurotics and enthusiasts. Then there are those coming to see people off, sadly perhaps, or to meet them. I hope the next time we see each other it's in a living room, gabbing over coffee, planning something normal like going to the movies. We've always lived this way, Márgara. Change is healthy. What about David?

"I told him not to come."

"Clearly. And?"

"He says he'll come and find me in a month."

"Where?"

"I'll be at home working a new job. It's time."

"Does he know all that?"

"No."

"You're crazy. You're just planning to throw away a catch like that?"

"He might be everything you say he is, but what he isn't is predictable. There's something of the frustrated adventurer in him, he's attracted to impossible tasks. He told me a story you know, the one about great-grandpa that you didn't hear. It was nothing but a litany of grand failures. My sense was that deep down he was telling about some utopian alter ego of his, the one he'd liked to have been.

Maybe not in the West, but out in some imaginary territory where men run crazy risks and fall hopelessly in love with fearless women. His invisible sister is one of them, you know? A modern Amazon, living among guerrillas and refugees. And there's David, determined right down to his core to slay an imaginary dragon and rescue her. I'm not a member of that heroic race. But I suppose if he wants a mission, not an impossible mission, mind you, maybe just an inconvenient one, I'll give it to him. It's mediocre and bureaucratic, nothing more than searching for addresses and consulting phone books. But it will let him, in his words, feel like an errant knight."

"Pretty complicated. Nothing like that would ever have occurred to me."

"Tell me, would you follow Bobby if he were to take a job in some Podunk town?"

"What a question. How would I know?"

"You know you and David have something in common. But I can't give him a real adventure like Bobby gives you. I guess the least I can do is make him use his imagination."

Camila lingers a moment more, contemplating the plane that's about to carry her sister away. Imagination. Rational to the last.

This Tuesday is almost like a Monday, where you're trying to recover your energy after a long weekend. Or is it that five days just aren't enough to get your brain around a new job? Márgara turns the faucet on to fill the tub and leans out the bathroom door to think, as she does so many times a day, about her apartment. It's not new like the job. But she came back obsessed with getting rid of her old things and all her old color schemes. She mercilessly gave away and threw away, then rearranged the rest. It looks like somebody dumped a barrel of white paint in here. The light from the desk lamps shines from one side of the apartment to the other without hitting or being slowed down by anything. The Buddha is the only thing with any presence, sitting there lording over a realm. She found him in the middle of the living room when she got back, the crate nearly took up the whole place. On it was a note from Bobby that read: Camila says even though you despise Malraux this thing is yours. His eyes follow her around at night, but not to worry, he's friendly.

Wrapped in a bathrobe (also white), her hair damp, she makes herself a whiskey with lots of ice and some water. She goes to turn on the television and hesitates a little. With luck one of those old movies she likes might be on. Instead she picks out some music and a book she started a few days back (she never got past the first few pages). She makes herself comfortable on the sofa, opens the book, and little by little dozes off. Something interrupts the melody, a noise that first gets mixed up with a dream, but eventually brings her back to reality. The doorbell. That damn stubborn doorbell. She leaves the book lying on the floor and gets up to answer it.

About the Author

Cecilia Urbina was born in Mexico City, where she grew up and now resides. She studied English and French literature at the Sorbonne and Cambridge University. She is the Coordinator of the Literature Department at Casa Lamm, where she teaches literature and creative writing. Her fields of study are contemporary British authors and postcolonial literature. She has written extensively in newspapers and cultural magazines. She has published six novels, including *Firme compañera* (Tava, 1994), *La imaginación de Roger Donal* (Sansores & Aljure, 1998), *De noche llegan* (Times Editores, 1999), and *Un martes como hoy* (Fondo de Cultura Económica, 2004), as well as a book of essays on contemporary writers, *De escritos y escritores* (Universidad Autónoma Metropolitana, 2001). In 2008, Cecilia Urbina received the prestigious Premio Coatlicue in recognition of *De noche llegan* and *Un martes como hoy*. She is married, and has three children.

About the Translator

Clare Sullivan is a teacher and translator who lives in Louisville, Kentucky. A faculty member in the Classical and Modern Languages Department of the University of Louisville, she earned her Ph.D. in Spanish from New York University in 2001. Sullivan's translation of Alicia Kozameh's novel, *259 saltos, uno inmortal,* was published as *259 Leaps, the Last Immortal* (Wings, 2007).

Wings Press was founded in 1975 by Joanie Whitebird and Joseph F. Lomax, both deceased, as "an informal association of artists and cultural mythologists dedicated to the preservation of the literature of the nation of Texas." Publisher, editor and designer since 1995, Bryce Milligan is honored to carry on and expand that mission to include the finest in American writing – meaning all of the Americas, without commercial considerations clouding the choice to publish or not to publish. Technically a "for profit" press, Wings receives only occasional underwriting from individuals and institutions who wish to support our vision. For this we are very grateful.

Wings Press attempts to produce multicultural books, chapbooks, CDs, DVDs and broadsides that, we hope, enlighten the human spirit and enliven the mind. Everyone ever associated with Wings has been or is a writer, and we know well that writing is a trans- formational art form capable of changing the world, primarily by allowing us to glimpse something of each other's souls. Good writing is innovative, insightful, and interesting. But most of all it is honest.

Likewise, Wings Press is committed to treating the planet itself as a partner. Thus the press uses as much recycled material as possible, from the paper on which the books are printed to the boxes in which they are shipped.

Associate editor Robert Bonazzi is also an old hand in the small press world. Bonazzi was the editor and publisher of Latitudes Press (1966-2000). Bonazzi and Milligan share a commitment to independent publishing and have collaborated on numerous projects over the past 25 years.

As Robert Dana wrote in *Against the Grain,* "Small press publishing is personal publishing. In essence, it's a matter of personal vision, personal taste and courage, and personal friendships." Welcome to our world.

Colophon

This first edition of *A Tuesday Like Today*, by Cecilia Urbina, has been printed on 70 pound paper containing fifty percent recycled fiber. Titles have been set in Papyrus type, the text is in Adobe Caslon type. All Wings Press books are designed and produced by Bryce Milligan.

On-line catalogue and ordering
available at
www.wingspress.com

Wings Press titles are distributed
to the trade by the
Independent Publishers Group
www.ipgbook.com